Introduction

"...to generally further the development of science fiction and allied arts, and of the communities surrounding it."

This quotation is taken from the British Science Fiction Association's constitution is a core principle of what we do. You can find the full document on our website – http://www.bsfa.co.uk

As part of that remit, I am pleased and proud to present the inaugural edition of Fission our new anthology publication which will be produced annually to join the rest of the BSFA's family of publications – *Vector*, *Focus* and *BSFA Review*. The remit of *Fission* is to develop both science fiction in general by publishing a selection of works, but also to add to the BSFA's work in developing science fiction writers. It is our hope that *Fission* will provide a pathway for

BSFA members, particularly those engaged with our Orbiter writing groups, towards getting their work 'out there' and assist them in developing their profiles as writers.

Fission #1 brings together a selection of excellent science fiction short stories which we are honoured to bring to you, the BSFA membership.

Each writer included in the anthology is on a different path and arrives here at a different stage in their career. We hope that your introduction to them, through us, will give you as a reader an opportunity to discover their other works which may aready be published or be forthcoming later. It might be that you already know one or two names from the list of authors, but I am sure you will discover more in our anthology, and I hope that each impresses you as they have impressed me when I accepted their submissions and put together this anthology.

Additionally, the BSFA is honoured to be partnering with Celsius. *Celsius 232* will feature a Spanish translation of 'Lyonesses' by So Mayer, whilst Fission #1 features an English translation of 'The Lego Calf' by Jon Bilbao.

I hope you enjoy the anthology.

Allen Stroud

Chair of the British Science Fiction Association.

The Aminals Marched in Two by Two
By Fatima Taqvi

It was all that homeschooling what started it. Or do I mean online learning? Can't really tell the difference. I was always too scared to open my mouth at the meetings. Easier to stay on mute.

We were all being driven out of our minds back then, weren't we? All us parents. Nobody could have anticipated it.

Having to do it all. Of course, the teachers tried their best but how can anyone through those screens? Can't connect over that, can you? Not really.

It was all holograms at first. Simple enough, but oh, did the little ones love it! Would have made your heart sing. Picture this – an English woodland. At the threshold between two very large oak trees, little animals jump and swing and chirrup and bleat. Singing songs together. Clapping

enthusiastically for each child who passed through.

Our Stacey couldn't get enough of it.

"Mum!" She looked up at me, mouth wide open. "Are we inside a cartoon?"

Every day they started with breathing exercises and a song. Then came stretches and games. And then a day with learning incorporated with everything outdoors. *We'll be okay*, I'd think, seeing everyone's faces, absorbed in their physics experiments dropping things from trees, moving on to arithmetic, adding up fallen acorns. *No. Better than okay.*

Each child got their own set of "aminals" as Stacey and Brian would say. A little apart from each other – still staying safe. But still a community. Still connected.

Brian had been a little wary, if I had to be honest with you. He'd had the worst of it. So little, and with no playmates, no nursery. No socialisation, you know? I could've sent him I suppose. Other people did. But there was always a bunch of us that couldn't bring ourselves to. Not with everything that was going on. Much better, we'd thought, to use these new schools. Even though they'd come

a little late for the very small ones.

So yes, Brian cringed a bit away from Rabbit and Snail and Squirrel and Duck. He even looked away from Strawberry Finch who was such a delightfully bright pink, I would have happily stayed myself.

"Now, Brian," I said, disentangling myself. "Let's play, just like your big sister."

"Don't like it," he whispered, looking at me with those big eyes. "Don't like *them*."

That decided me, the whispering. The fact that he couldn't just abandon his inhibitions and join in like the other little ones. I couldn't let him go on like this. Whispering. Flinching from faces. I did what they advised us to, and sat a little away with a firm, happy smile as he cried quietly in a corner.

Ah, it did the rest of them a world of good, I can tell you that. They'd been cooped up for ages. Not to mention all the mental health issues we'd started seeing. Remember the loneliness? How cut off we'd become?

"Sign me up for one of those forest schools," I'd joke with the other Mums as the children came tearing out, shrieking and full of high spirits, dead leaves in their hair and holes in their socks. Not that I ever stuck

around. After the first week, once I'd dropped the kids off, I'd sit outside a coffee shop, crack open a laptop and cry my heart out while pretending to work.

I couldn't stop crying, it seemed. Life wasn't the same. It was going on all around me, but a part of it wasn't going to come back. I couldn't put my finger on what it was. I just knew it was gone. We'd been through a phase of time that not only connected a before and an after but had warped them both beyond recognition. The past was more memorable. The future, less savoury. Not to mention underfunded.

Anyway, like I said, first it was holograms, then it got really sophisticated. The teachers who used to hang about in the background got their own sim overlays. Now they also looked like... anything they wanted to. So, they could all be dinosaurs, for example, and the children would run around with them through the forests. Any given morning you could hear screams of laughter, and running, and you could see the children shimmying up trees to pelt each other with acorns.

Gone forever were the school bells and

dinner ladies. No more PE shoes, and certainly no more uniforms. Now it was the forests and beaches and meadows. Over in Scotland and Wales we heard even the mountains were popular learning spots.

A year later, and the educational psychologists wanted in. So, you had your groups saying children shouldn't be learning that animals sing, since that wasn't natural. And they tinkered with that, gave the holograms more natural animal behaviours. Then you had some saying the children should be learning how to farm now that all the workers had either been deported or had died.

Some said it was fun for a while, but were we really going to do away completely with concrete buildings? This was a little late in the day for that argument, but you know what they're like. They pretend they know everything, when actually the world has moved on long ago.

In the end the whole thing evolved to the point that we had little AIs programmed to teach - sorry, *facilitate learning* - for children of all ages. Every day you could hear them, screaming with joy. Splashing in rivers in the summer, making fires in the winter.

I shouldn't have kept going off to the coffee shop.

"So, what do they all actually learn?" My parents would ask me on video chat.

Typical, I'd think. Some of us just can't move on with the times.

"The important thing," I said, "is the children are happy! They're out in the open air! Learning real things close to nature. You can't teach that in a classroom."

One of the other mums was like that. Kept asking, who was it coming up with the tech for these things? Forwarding us really long articles I didn't have the time to read.

"They're supposed to mirror the kids, so they feel accepted. Reflect back body language. Emotions. There's an algorithm to it. So, who's coming up with all of it?" She'd hiss at us. "Who's paying for it? This is warfare technology."

Soon she'd pulled her kid out and stopped coming. I think she moved away. Far away.

One day I saw my Stacey climbing up a tree barefoot. Now why does that worry me? I thought. Because it did. It wasn't like her usual self. It was like seeing a different child altogether. Then when I thought about it I

realised it had been ages since I'd seen her scream at a spider or refuse to eat her broccoli.

Fay and Henry, the only grandparents in our circle, weren't happy at all.

"It's not good for them," Fay said. Henry nodded. They were squashed together, bunches of pink and white pixels moving on the screen.

"Children are savages," he added. "They have to be led with force. With strength. If you give them up to nature, they've no... no alpha."

"What do you mean?" I leaned forward. "Like wolves?"

"Like children," he said, his voice steel. "Children are devils. They do the work of becoming civilised in growing up. They need leaders."

"Oh, you see now," Pat stirred, the screen taking up her face now. "That's such a Eurocentric construct. Very out of touch with how other cultures view it. Children are innocents. Dear little things."

"Doesn't mean they don't need a leader."

Lauren's Viv brought a dead squirrel home. Said she planned on skinning it and using the fur as a hat. Very sensible, the

teachers responded when Lauren complained. Fewer teachers now than when we'd started. They just didn't need that many anymore. Efficient, you see. Small group learning. The ones that were left, I have to say, looked a little odd. They'd taken to carrying around the smaller AIs on their shoulders. The smiling teacher watching the children leave when I'd come to pick up Stacey and Brian had chosen crows. They'd sit on her shoulders, glittering eyes watching us, cawing in unison over Stacey's chatter.

Joyce's Amy didn't eat anything from home anymore. Days and days went by. Her mother begged her to tell her what she was eating. Turns out she'd been foraging food in the forest. They'd all been. I found squashed insects in Stacey's pockets. And mushrooms, which worried me.

"That's not poisonous," Stacey told me when I freaked out at her. "Nothing to worry about."

The children were going hunting. Some even stalked deer, which I don't think they're supposed to. They picked wild fruit. Stole library books about poisonous plants.

I don't suppose we'd have made so much

information free if we'd known people would actually use it.

We did a town meeting to discuss it all. At a barn. Open air as much as it could be, because the dangers otherwise weren't quite passed. It was nice, getting together. Bringing food. Discussing things about our children. Being parents.

A roar, and the doors flung themselves open, swinging back and forth.

"Bloody wind," Pat said, without turning around from the thermos. Five cups were filled with tea in front of her. She was pouring a sixth.

A strawberry finch flew in. Two of them.

They sat on Pat's shoulders.

Two squirrels scurried in and sat on opposite sides of me.

"Have they always been that big?" I murmured.

A crow cawed. The tea crashed to the floor as the table was flipped over.

Henry sighed as two snails flanked him. It was a sweet sound, I thought later, like when the credits are about to begin after your favourite film. He said something I couldn't catch.

"Sorry?"

"They have weapons."

That's when the children came running in. And yes. They did.

Outside in the dark the other AIs made a ring around the building.

"Aminals," Stacey said fondly, slipping her grubby hand into mine as she led me out of the ring. But the ring they made was otherwise a firm and non-negotiable one, as a few people found out as they tried to break through and escape. Flashes of light, and the smell of burnt flesh.

"We will all live in the wild, Mummy," Stacey said, smiling up at me. "Just like people in the old days. We'll do real things like catching furry animals and going splashing in rivers. And you can't say no because it's too late, you see. I'm me now."

"Alright, sweetie," I said. "Alright."

"Carla drowned the other day." Stacey stepped over a rock that I stubbed my toe on. "She went into the water and couldn't come out. It was so sad, but then we built a little house for her ghost, and now she loves us and blesses the waters and we sing a song to her everyday just for luck. But it's all real,

Contents

GW01511243

Fi:

An Anthology of Stories from the British Science Fiction Association

http://www.bsfa.co.uk

Fission #1.

First published in the UK in 2021 by the British Science Fiction Association (BSFA) & HWS Press

ISBN: 978-1-910987-96-4

Mummy. More real than assemblies. And we don't have to listen to anybody. Wouldn't you like that? And the aminals say we can even put anyone who doesn't listen to them in jail. I know how to tie all the knots!"

A few feet away some of the AIs were dragging the ones still resisting outside.

"But why do we have to, love?" I tried to reason with her. "What's wrong with our house? Wait… Where's Brian?"

Stacey made a face. "The Aminals say he'll come join us later. They all will. All the children. It'll just be too much fun to stay away."

There was nothing else to be done.

I'm sitting here, under an oak tree. I've shaved my head. You can still use bathroom facilities, but I suppose I've just thrown myself into the lifestyle. I have to say, I'm so proud of my Stacey. My daughter is brown bodied. Strong. Muscular. She eats all her venison and helps clean all the bones. All by herself. She has a sense of importance, you know? She doesn't whine anymore, and she doesn't throw fits at supermarkets in front of the toy section. She plays with acorns and pinecones and scrapes bark off the trees with her friends, painting a new language of shapes and symbols on the trees with mud.

Once I saw a small, thin face peering at me from behind a tree. It was covered in dirt and was being very careful to stay hidden.

I looked at Brian, and he looked at me. Then, after what seemed like hours, he turned around in reluctance, and went away.

I hope he comes to see me again soon.

The children have been picking wild bramble berries. Stacey took a couple out of her mouth when they came back and slipped one to me. The rest would be used to make a tart, with all the children pitching in, laughing and helping each other.

You can't teach that in a classroom.

A Pall of Moondust
By Nick Wood

KwaZulu Natal, African Federation, 2035.

Blue sky: red dust.

Hamba kahle, grandfather, goodbye.

I sprinkled a handful of orange-red dust on his grave - yet another funeral cloth over your buried body, Babamkhulu – and, behind me, father did the same.

May your soul soar, old man with the sharp tongue and that mad dog, Inja.

And say hello to mother for me.

*

Shackleton Crater, Moon Base One, Lunar, 2037

I dreamed, and shook awake, as the two bodies flew away from me. Dreams live.

Scott is the one keying in the Airlock code, mouth O-ing in shock at the tug and hiss of escaping air behind her. "Helmets on," she says, but it is already too late, the door to the Moon behind her wide as a monster's maw.

Bailey is fiddling with the solar array on the Rover, his helmet playfully dangled on the joystick for a second, before being sucked out and beyond my reach.

Scott pushes me backwards and the inner door closes, leaving me safe on the inside. The wrong side?

The Airlock explodes with emptying air and a spray of moon dust.

Two die, while I live.

I scoured the darkness for something familiar, something safe.

Nothing.

I'm a lunar newbie, only Three Lunar Walks in and with my helmet already on, before we had even entered the airlock. That's mandatory now - helmet must be on, before airlock entry. Why then, does this darkness hang so heavy with my guilt?

Medication drooped my eyelids, pulling me back towards the faulty doors and O-ing mouths, where I did not want to go.

No, not again, please…

*

Doctor Izmay eyed me over her desk-screen, and I yawned back at her, glancing at the red couch in the corner of her room labelled 'Sector 12 Psych'. The bed is a cliché, surely, just for show?

"Flashbacks still, Doctor Matlala?" she asked, raising a sympathetic eyebrow.

Her formality reminded me of father, but Izmay was a real woman of everywhere, German/Turkish/North African, a true shrink of the world.

I don't like shrinks.

But I had been taught well and avoided direct gaze with my elder, a swarthy white woman greying at the temples, of her tightly bunned black hair.

She smiled. "Ah, a mark of respect for those older than you, in traditional Zulu custom."

Her eyes were grey-green, I stared in surprise.

"Like you, young woman, I do my homework," she said, "Do we need to titrate your medication and increase your dose?"

I hesitated. "I want to get back to my work in hydroponics, but the medication is making me drowsy."

"There's something else you need to do first." The woman leaned back, hesitant too, and dread surged inside me again. "You need to suit up and go back out onto the Moon."

"Uh – no. What's the point? I'm a botanist. Nothing grows out there."

The psychiatrist stood and walked towards the door, gesturing me to follow. "Necessary health and safety. You know the drill. We must all get comfortable on the surface of this Harsh Mistress. For you, that means getting back on your metaphorical horse and into the Airlock, just for starters."

I could not stand; my limbs were locked.

Doctor Izmay hauled out an injection pen and sighed, tapping it on her palm. "I agree. Your medication does need increasing."

*

The psychiatrist held my arm firmly as we approached the airlock door and I was grateful for that, my legs starting to jelly.

"Slow your breathing," she said sharply. "Think of Durban beach."

I practiced our imagery work, heading

into my safe mind-space, as she counted out a slowed pace for my breath. Hot white-yellow sand, pumping surf, blue bottle jelly fish and…sharks in the water?

"Helmet on," she said, but the airlock door in front of us was gaping like the jaws of a Great White.

I tripped over the two bodies they had brought back.

Scott and Bailey, suited and helmetless, darkened by a coat of regolith, with their eye sockets and tongues caked in the black dust that was everywhere.

"Stay with me, Thandike," a voice said, "Breathe, one…two…"

But I have dropped the helmet, in case it sucks me out.

I bend with suited difficulty, scraping the floor for moon dust that stinks like weak gunpowder, so as to sprinkle it respectfully on the bodies of Scott and Bailey.

So little to scoop up, so little to leave them in peace. Why is it just I who live still?

My eyes leaked with sorrow and guilt, so that I hardly felt yet another injection into my upper arm.

Where have their bodies gone? And are

their shades happy?

*

"Survivor guilt is normal," Doctor Izmay told me.

This time she had me lying on her red leather couch, so that I did not have to look at her eyes. "You could have done nothing differently. It's not your fault."

Yes, I know that, so why do I still feel guilty?

"Tell me about your grandfather."

The command dropped onto my stomach like a lead weight. Even in Moon gravity, it felt heavy. I prefer plants to words, any day.

"He helped father raise me, after my mother died, when I was very young," I struggled to hold my tears in. "He died at ninety, the year before I got into the Lunar Programme. I wish I could have shown him my letter of acceptance."

"You still miss him?" Her voice was nearer, as if she'd shifted closer to me, on the seat behind the couch.

It's an obvious question, so I did not even bother to respond.

"Tell me more about him," Dr. Izmay tried again. "What do you miss the most?"

"No," I said. "It has no relevance here. I need to get back to the issue of efficient grain production in one sixth gee and filtered sunlight."

A noise clicked from behind the red couch, now sticky with stale sweat from my back. Above me, the ceiling slid open and I saw a window funnelled to the roof of the dome. Sharp stars cut down into my eyes, lancing slivers of light, with no atmospheric distortion to turn them twinkle friendly.

"The light from those stars is variously between four hundred and five billion years old," Dr. Izmay said. "They will fade with Earthrise imminent, but they won't disappear. They're still there, even when they're gone. Tell me about your grandfather."

"No," I said, eyes burning, so that I screwed them shut. Stars are like my grandfather? Could I have been quicker to call 9-1-1, when his heart collapsed that day?

"You've always done your best," Dr. Izmay's voice was even closer still. "In the end, with death, we can change nothing."

I opened my eyes and twitched with

shock. She was bending over me from the back of the couch, eyes fastened on mine: "What was your grandfather's favourite phrase, when you were a teenager?"

"Get off that bloody couch and do something useful, intombi!" The words were out of my mouth, before I could think.

Dr. Izmay was laughing, "Well?"

She had done her homework on me, very well indeed.

*

Today, my two moon-walking companions were to be Commander Baines and Space Tourist Butcher.

I had checked the records on both, the night before.

Baines had over four hundred walks under his buckled belt and had slid like a snake into his own suit, although bending stiffly to pick up his helmet and gloves. "I've got me your bio-signs on my screen visor here, so I'm keeping tabs on both of you. We're not going far. Just keep me in sight and do everything I tell you. Helmets on."

My heart pumped a surge of panic, but

Butcher looked even more terrified.

It's his first time, at the ancient age of forty-six. I'm not the newest newbie here.

"Just breathe slowly," I told him. "Don't hyperventilate into your mouthpiece."

Dr. Izmay crackled into my ears as I fasten my helmet on. "Good. I'm patched in from remote too, Thandike. Looks like I might have to copyright that breathing line."

My chuckle took the edge off my dread.

Baines was already thumbing in the access code and I took up my position at the back. (Newbie in the middle, yet another reg. change, since the accident.)

"Fool proof new locking system," says Baines, bouncing through the opening airlock door.

Butcher followed, more slowly and clumsily.

I stepped forward to support his PLSS backpack, preventing the novice from toppling backwards - as he momentarily backed away from the door, as if having had sudden second thoughts.

I may only be twenty-eight, but I know by now, that nothing is ever fool proof… So what the hell am I doing stepping through this door myself?

It's better than going home, for a start. It's taken me a long time and lots of hard work to get here, ahead of so much global competition. And, now that I'm here, I'm going to make sure I stay off that bloody couch. For you, Babamkhulu.

The door behind me closed and Baines was already busy on the external door, as if minimising our chances for anxiety to escalate. "Butcher, breathe, one, two…" I said, hearing a quick rasping in my ears.

"Ready for exit, decompression complete."

Slowly, the outer door opened.

Hesitantly, we followed Baines' loping bounce out onto the surface of the moon.

We needed to step upwards slightly, as the door has been built low into a crater wall, to minimise solar radiation exposure.

I strode across to a large boulder to my right, keeping Baines in view. How can it look so dark, with such a bright sun?

Baines was a few steps further along, by a mound of broken rocks. He moves so quickly, as if he doesn't even think about the steps he has left behind.

“Both of you; take a look at that!" Baines’ voice crackled as he raised an arm to point, along the horizon to our right.

The Earth shimmered low over the horizon – a largish blue-white ball floating above the lip of Shackleton's crater, where solar arrays in eternal sunlight bled back cheap and climate friendly energy to the planet.

I focused on Earth. Where are the continents? Where is Africa?

The blur of grey-white cloud smeared the blue-green oceans and brown earth across the globe. I could almost hear it spinning, swirling hot climate clouds across the face of the world.

It doesn’t matter if I can’t find Africa. From here, nothing is ‘Great’, nothing is ‘Permanent’. For all of us humans alike, we have a melting, fragile pearl to protect.

“And look there!” Baines swivelled to point at the sky behind us.

I turned to peer – in the deep darkness, where the stars were fading, a dull reddish pinprick burned.

“Mars, our next stop, ” said Baines.

The colour of the earth, with which we

had covered grandfather.

Butcher and Baines continued to watch Mars, but I stared back at the sealed crater door. No, surely not?

"What's happening to your pulse and breathing, Thandike?" Dr. Izmay's voice bit into my ear.

I raise a gloved hand to take the edge off the solar glare. On the top-edge of the crater, near the dome roof, sat an old man with a knobkierie stick, with a dog by his side.

I knew better than to say anything, but walked back to Base slowly, testing my vision. The old man stood to wave and his voice quavered to me, across the vacuum: "Proud to see you doing something so special and useful, umzukulu!"

Two space-suited figures hovered behind him. They waved once.

Inja barked, and – when I blinked again – all of them had gone.

They had warned me to expect visual distortions in this alien land, where distance and depth were hard to judge, and the shifting shadows played with your perception.

"What did you see, Thandike?" Doctor Izmay's voice echoed into my ears.

I hesitated… "Our home crater and the outer door."

I said a prayer, silently.

I watched the soon to disappear stars above me, as sun rise approaches, to break the shorter lunar night.

Behind me, Baines and Butcher have arrived, but I finish my prayer.

*

Cunjani, grandfather, hello. Your soul has soared to the Moon itself; I see.

So, tell me, how is my mother?

Black sky: grey dust. Inyanga, 2037

Ends

Wanderlust
By Eugen Bacon & E. Don Harpe

"LAPIS LAZULI," sie says. "That my name."

Sie's not of this world, never from Earth. Not with those eyes, no.

Sie sits next to me, chewing popcorn and laughing, laughing, laughing at the jokes of a stand-up artist at the pub. The comedian is doing a 'Who is this somebody?' feature, rolling on a new gig, a Bill Clinton impersonation that works so well it warms patrons with mirth on this night of howling storm.

The performance is a rib-tickler, so funny it almost brings the house down. And the decidedly iridescent alien beside me laughs vigorously along with the rest of us.

An alien? you quiz. Surely, but not what you think.

Sie's not odious, not at all. Hir mouth is sensual, petal-shaped and just as hued. Sie's an insightful creature, I can tell, one to be handled with care if I'm to get any closer. Sie moves about in a playful way, secure in hir mirth, comfortable with hir surrounding, accepting it, not once questioning the patrons or the bar itself, or even me.

I stop looking at the black guy on the dais, as he impersonates poor Bill choking on a red-hot chilli pepper regurgitated by a femme fatale in the heart of a kiss and find myself admiring Lapis. Sure, hir skin refracts light. It gives sie this radiant hue that outshines anything I've seen. In the deepest throes of laughter sie pales yet does so without losing radiance.

You wonder at my taste, my intention … But it's not customary for specimens of this ilk to show up in a pub, let alone this one. Sie's desirable, really, an aroma of roses and petunia, I just wanted to take sie home.

When a Greek ambassador in the act catches Bill with his pants down, and his enchantress crashes out of a window swinging on a curtain, Lapis turns a deep, dark blue with big, ivory veins.

An hour later, I ask why sie's still laughing, the comedy act is done.

"I not be laughing," sie chokes. "These be

my tears. I am inversion, not me real."

"What inversion?" I say. "How is this not the real you?"

Turns out sie was arrested for a trumped-up charge, found guilty in a hasty court, sentenced to banishment from the land of Magnetroxis. Hir molecules were refracted, turned sie inside out.

Sie no more resembles any of hir kind. Sie wanders the universe, floats alone, laughs when sie should cry, craving hir *lazurite*.

"What is your *lazurite*?" I ask, wanting yet not wanting to know.

"The half of my rib," sie says, "bearer of my unborn child."

"Alas!" I say. "I thought you were…?"

"Lapis Lazuli. That my name. Who be you think?"

"Never mind. But banished? Why?"

Sie turns upon me opaque eyes ingrained with gold, eyes so full of personal appeal I want to gather sie to my chest, hold sie until those eyes shine with dawn.

"General Adrastea," sie sobs-cum-chuckles. "Me feel no love, not love sie back. I already get my *lazurite*, see."

"But how did you get here? Earth?"

A clap of thunder, sie says. Polarised hir fragments to shape them into the form sie's now. Having lost transportability, sie flittered onto the seat sie's sat upon, and it was I, hir first Earth people, who leaned forward to give sie food.

"Popdibles," sie says.

"Popcorn," I correct. "And what will become of sie? Your *lazurite*?"

Sie shared hir eternal fate. Sie would carry the little one in hir womb until the punishment is complete. Then, only then, will they once more unite back home in Magnetroxis.

I stare in silence, fled out of questions.

I do take sie home. Not to surrender sie to the comfort of my lips, so sie might feel less lonely. I take sie to my home in a fierce tug of impulse to warm sie a glass of milk, to lace it with brandy and cover sie with a blanket until sie stops laughing laughing…

Crying.

When the storm calms, I take sie out to the woods beneath a sky full of blackness where, without looking back, sie leaps!

My hair madly billows like a cloak in the consequent wind of hir flight. I clasp my longing in tight palms. Pining ripples me inside out. I defy logic by needing sie, but I do, and already I miss sie.

Lapis, dear Lazuli.

I watch sie open up miles from me and then dissipate. Dissolve into big and then smaller bubbles that float the behemoth sky. The eaves of a big black cloud yawn to swallow the bubbles, drag forlorn Lapis and the pieces of my heart to a world I cannot inhabit, to a future without me. Back to intergalactic wilderness, to voices in the wind, where sie would carry hir wanderlust to the end of hir banishment.

The Blood Between Us
by Katherine Franklin

Forun

Given that now should be my first holiday in two decades, I hadn't expected to see the galactic core again so soon. Yet here I am, watching through the murk of my stabilising gel tank as the great, open plains of the outer sphere rise into view. My back itches where my skin folds over into a hood, heavy with spore that I should be releasing on Parihan at this very moment. But Parihan is a long way from the core, and murder compels me to travel here.

I slide forwards in the tank to view the projections displayed on the chitin-glass. The thought image that called me here fluctuates in three shallow dimensions, parsing its details into the space available: a sentient murdered, the suspect nowhere to be found. In ordinary circumstances such a murder would not merit my involvement. These are not ordinary circumstances.

"We have arrived, Mediator Forun," says the shuttle's pilot, his species' characteristic slurping drawl just distinguishable behind translation.

"My thanks."

I wait for the gel to drain through the floor grates before opening the door and gliding out, past the rest of the empty passenger area to the bright square of sky by the open hatch. A gust of cool air sets my skin tingling, moisture evaporating from its surface. I extend masses of external gills to catch the breeze, then descend the ramp.

It is a drama. I heard these crowds shouting nearby the moment the gel slipped away. Crowds shouting means discontent, no doubt related to my latest investigation. Crowds are a mess we do not have the time to deal with. So, I make myself big, and impressive, and if the sound does not abate as I exit, I do at least see those nearest the shuttle part to let me pass. They have respect for mediators and recognise a Parhiaan of my age and influence.

A Clik-tik awaits me at the bottom of the ramp, his mouthparts the only part of his body revealed by his weaponised shell. They part as I approach. I do not recognise the expression – as mediation protocol demands, I have no prior experience with his species, nor with humans.

"You are security personnel?" I ask.

He drums a note on his chest with a pincer, which the translator marks as affirmative.

I sweep past him and gesture at the crowds. They hold holographic placards that flicker with text and crude depictions of fleshy bipeds. "Care to explain how the public has gained knowledge of this investigation?"

Metal-tipped legs clatter along the floor behind me. "Entirely our fault, mediator. My people found the body, heard who'd fled, got angry. Someone overheard."

"And now the entire hub has heard, no doubt. Do you greet me to tell me this? I am quite capable of locating the investigative offices myself, given I have spent the past fifty-five years within."

The Clik-tik's gait falters a moment, then resumes. "Was on my way to review the security footage. Docks were on the way."

Predictable. I turn, and the Clik-tik pulls up short to avoid ploughing into me. His mouthparts part. Pincers open and close.

"Your name?" I ask.

"Ka'Pe-ta."

"Ka'Pe-ta, you are not authorised further involvement in this case, as you should be aware by my presence."

"I—"

"If you would still be useful, find me the suspect and see a mob doesn't take their flesh. Can you do that?"

More slow motions, openings and closings, a foot raised then lowered. Then he gestures what must be another affirmative. With a series of clicks, he turns and heads back the way he came, into the bulk of the crowd. I turn back to my path, and to the job ahead of me.

*

"I need details."

The investigative attaché blinks up from its desk, the great round eyes that make up most of its body wide and staring. It chirps a short, "Which?"

"State of the victim upon discovery. State of the location. Details of who discovered the scene and which security officers are involved from each species. Then I require the footage."

Another blink, and just like that my implants flag up a download on my wrapscreen. I pass through a short corridor into the familiar dim space of my office, then unfurl the screen from around one of my tendrils and examine it. Ka'Pe-ta told the truth. His people heard a disturbance, found the body and gave failed chase to an escaping human. They have marked the body's initial condition simply as 'murdered', and beyond that I will have to wait for results from autopsy. Humanity's slim presence on the hub found out with Clik'tik officers almost breaking down their door, and have assigned Charise Bentham, their only security officer, to the case. She, at least, has not seen fit to disturb me. Perhaps humans know the air they float upon is thin.

I load the security footage through a sensory filter and wait for it to be ready. An empty room appears, frozen in time. I check its registration against the database, find it's a hired room, booked by the victim. At first this seems noteworthy, but a quick check into Clik-tik behaviours indicates it is usual. They sleep in their shells in communal areas. For anything private – more private than the confines of their shells – they seek wilderness. Where there is none, they hire some. A burgeoning industry on the hub.

I let time unfreeze. A human enters, shifting all about the room on his spindly legs, brushing at the long, dark filaments that cup all but the front circle of his head. The system identifies him as Shameel Farid, assistant to the human representative. An incendiary suspect for murder, to be sure.

P'Xacti 80-2-18 enters. As soon as he does, Shameel rushes at him, does something indistinguishable at this angle, then retreats. P'Xacti leaps in pursuit and in one bound has Shameel pinned against the wall. I watch, astounded, expecting the human to fall beneath natural advantage, but as the two squirm, he dodges anything fatal. More astounding still, he fumbles at the Clik-tik's shell and at last has it open. P'Xacti trembles out from his armoured strength only to fall straight into the human's grasp. Shameel bludgeons it for just over a minute before P'Xacti starts to fit. His legs spasm and he hurtles across the room, separating from Shameel and staying so until he twitches his last.

Shameel walks to P'Xacti's body and rocks it with a limb, checking to see if he is dead. Then his head whips around to face the door and he fumbles with his attire before darting out of the back entrance.

Peculiar.

"Attaché?" I call through on the intercom. "What do you have on movements for both suspect and victim in the days leading up to the incident?"

*

Charise

I hammer at the door again, feeling the eyes of a crowd accumulating in the street behind me. "Open up!"

"Officer Bentham," comes a tinny voice through the door's speaker. "Please bear with us. The embassy's closed until it can issue—"

"I don't care if it's shitting closed; it's not

closed to me. Let me in." I curl my hands around the grip of my pistol, squeezing it tight as I resist the urge to kick the door. They build them sturdy enough that it wouldn't burst open, but it might be satisfying.

One year. Humanity gets welcomed into the galactic community and just one year later, we've already gone and fucking blown it. Murder. Bastard, whoever did it, and half a bastard whoever stops me getting to him. I draw my hand back to knock again.

"Is there some trouble here?"

Shoulders tensing, I glance back. A Clik-tik's standing right behind me, in pincer-grabbing range, optics glowing from the end of the components that shield their eye stalks. There's a badge stamped on their shell where it slopes back above their eyes. Security. Same badge as mine. I bristle but try to hide it. Good thing we're new enough that no one's used to our body language yet. I've never been good at faking.

"It's a human issue," I say. "I'm handling it."

Their mouthparts twitch. "No doubt. But I need to speak with your diplomat regarding the death of P'Xacti 80-2-18. As the suspect's employer, she may have useful information."

I chew at my lip, glaring at the door and willing it to open. "His whereabouts are a human concern. I'll find him. And when I do, I'll fucking kill him myself."

"That would—"

"Speaking metaphorically," I say and sigh. "Not going to keep the bastard from trial."

It's a while before the Clik-tik responds. From their mouthparts' motion, I get the impression they're working out what to say next. Still nothing from the other side of the door. I'm wasting time.

"As one of ours is involved," they say, "I am within rights to pursue the suspect, the same as you. The mediator has tasked me with finding him."

That earns a snort. "Thought mediators're supposed to be impartial?"

"She just wants a swift resolution, and no further bloodshed."

I haven't been blind to the situation on the hub. A lot of people pissed at humans. A lot of places it's bad to go right now if you are one. "Fine. Two heads are better than one – we can both look for him. You got any leads from your people?"

"If I did, I wouldn't be here."

Fair enough. Turning, I pound on the door again.

"Officer—"

"It's extraofficial now. Mediator wants answers. That means we need to get in."

A pause. Then the door slides open, and the guard's tight-drawn face peers out around it. He ushers us in, his eyes flicking only briefly to the Clik-tik before settling on the crowd.

"Quickly," he says. "Dr Lasham's upstairs."

The Clik-tik thanks him, but I'm already gone, taking the thick-carpeted stairs three at a time. Metal-tipped footsteps behind me, keeping pace. At the top of the stairs, Dr Lasham appears from a side room, flustered, tucking brunette hair behind her implants.

"Officer? Officers," she corrects herself, "this way." She ushers us into another room, small, with little plump seats. She stands, leaning against a windowsill that overlooks the gardens. "Whatever it is you have to say, please make it quick. We're having to release a statement on recent events and any delay could have serious repercussions."

The Clik-tik beats me to the punch. "We need information on Shameel Farid's whereabouts and temperament prior to the incident, plus any indication you might have of his current location."

I wonder, idly, if he really makes his speech that formal or if it's the same treatment the translators give to everyone. Maybe he's flipping our diplomat the verbal bird, and no one understands to notice.

Dr Lasham sighs and shrugs. Seems tired. "I don't know what to say. I didn't know Shameel as well as I ought to. He was professional. Kept his personal life very much to himself, though he probably would have spoken if any of us had asked him. But he seemed content. Fulfilled. Other cultures fascinated him, and I think he went out of his way to find out as much about them as possible. So, to think he bent to murder... I can't reconcile that with my image of him."

People seldom can with murderers.

"Do you know where he might have gone?" I ask. Humanity's limited presence on the hub means there aren't many places to hide, unless you chance it with strangers.

None of those are going to be welcoming us any time soon.

"He liked the gardens. I sometimes walked past him after a long day, still sat on one of the benches."

"Hmm. Hardly a good place to hide."

But the Clik-tik taps a stiletto against the carpet. "P'Xacti worked in the gardens. Perhaps their paths crossed."

"Or perhaps someone closer to home found a way to keep him secret," I say. We searched his home, but his neighbours could be hiding something.

"Then there are two avenues, and two heads, as you say." The Clik-tik turns to me, lifting a mandible. "If I question P'Xacti's colleagues, will you search Shameel's friends?"

"Gladly," I say, and leave the diplomat's offices with Officer Ka'Pe-ta's contact details stored in my implants.

*

Forun

"Species-independent autopsy indicates a biotoxin, Mediator."

"Are you sure?" I have the security footage, the conversation, and the autopsy report open at once. A biotoxin indicates premeditation, but the attack – or its results – looked almost accidental. I ponder that for a second. "Could the toxin be endemic to humans? An allergic reaction to part of their physiology?"

"Not that we can tell without further investigation, or species-specific knowledge. Would you have us pursue one?"

I drift from one side of the room to the other, letting conditioned air flow across my hood. "I will send you the footage of the murder. If it gives you no further insight into how the toxin was administered, let me know, and I will permit a human doctor to review the case."

Satisfied, the doctor thanks me and returns to work. Spores itch all beneath my hood, and for the first time in hundreds of years, I feel impatience. There is good reason we seek independent judgment, but sometimes the lack of context is blinding. My species is sought after for such tasks because we can spend decades poring over a picture until it is right, but with the situation on the hub, decades aren't in the picture. I scratch at my hood with a tendril, feeling the spores' pressure to release.

Perhaps this one needs accelerating. When officers Bentham and Ka'Pe-ta return, I will show them the recording. They will no doubt make more inherent sense of it than I.

*

Charise

Ka'Pe-ta arrives at my position near the docks just as Shameel's body is being loaded into a transport for the morgue. The people loading it are Clik-tiks. Either they just happened to be on call, or their security personnel are jumping all over this case. Perhaps Ka'Pe-ta knows them. He stares after them, mouthparts moving silently, then turns his gaze in my direction.

"Murdered?" he asks.

"What does it matter? Problem's gone, one way or the other."

Though I don't understand his body language, I feel some weight behind his optics, judging me. Imagined, probably. Felt, nonetheless.

"It matters," he says, "because we do not have the answers. Justice must be followed to its conclusion, and the truth revealed with it."

I sigh. "Yeah, I know. We should probably take this back to the mediator, let her know what's happened. Walk with me?"

Ka'Pe-ta surveys the scene one more time, then clacks his chest. We move out onto the street together, a human and a Clik-tik side by side. Nothing of particular note until the murder. Now we get stares from the people lining the street. No humans there, just other species directing most of their anger at me. But there are Clik-tik, too. Two giant ones amongst them, twice the size of Ka'Pe-ta, and they fall into step behind us.

"Friends of yours?" I ask.

"Unlikely." His pace has stiffened, his joints flexing less with each step, making him appear taller.

"What's the mood like, with your people? You think this could have been revenge?"

"P'Xacti's shell hasn't been released for repurposing. As long as that is the case, there will be anger, and blame. I can't say whether revenge would have driven this. How did he die?"

'Hanged.'

'Hanged?'

I turn to face him as we walk and realise he really doesn't know what I mean. I consider what that implies for the likelihood of an alien murdering a human.

"I'll explain when we meet the mediator."

*

Forun

The suspect's death only convinces me that acceleration is the right decision. Leave this too long and two murders may become more. Officer Bentham is trying to tell me something, but whatever it is, she can wait. I lead the both of them to a viewing screen, lock the room and let the footage play.

They watch, intent, and as it plays out, I see their bodies morph from one unidentifiable expression into another.

When it reaches the part when P'Xacti is extracted from his shell, both of them recoil. The human raises an arm in front of her face and says, "Oh, no, no, stop!" Then at the same time as she says, "That's disgusting!", Ka'Pe-ta says "That's beautiful!"

Officer Bentham turns from the recording to face P'Xacti. "What?"

"What?"

"You said beautiful like it's a bad thing."

He gestures to the recording. "For the beauty of a body to be revealed... it is a private thing. Not for others to behold."

I pause the recording, though it is only a second from completion. "Explain."

The two officers look everywhere but at me, then Ka'Pe-ta says, "They were mating."

Several seconds pass before I ask, "Mating?"

"Yes. Willingly. Whatever caused the death, it was an accident."

Officer Bentham adds, "And Shameel wasn't murdered. He killed himself."

I turn to face the security footage, all the pieces falling into tragically obvious shape.

"Thank you," I say. "That will be all."

*

Charise

The gardens here are quiet, as if even the

birds want to listen in to whatever we have to say next.

"I don't think I could have pictured... *that* if I tried," Ka'Pe-ta says.

I clear my throat, trying hard to banish a well-established blush. "I'm surprised it worked."

"It very evidently did not."

I think about the Clik-tik, convulsing and dying on the floor, and the look on Shameel's face, and have to agree.

Etaerio
By Rosie Oliver

Being neat is worse than a fetish for me, more like a religion. I even iron my shirts when they come back from the cleaners to ensure they are crease-free. As for the chaos and mayhem other people leave in their wake, let's just say I had to take seven intensive courses of anger management. I can now overlook others' untidiness, though I find it extremely hard.

However, I can't ignore something I have to deal with every day, the English language. I cringe at all those missing commas, misplaced apostrophes and abhorrent foreign words that eject perfectly decent words from our vocablurary.

Thank goodness the Oxford English Dictionary has every word with its detailed derivation history. Most newer words result from technological advances and are easily grouped around core words, or as I prefer to think of them, kernels. An example is

aeroplane being the kernel
for *aviatrix*, *aeronautics* and *avionics*. These groups don't overlap, which makes me think of our technological language is like an aggregated fruit of drupes such as a raspberry or bunch of grapes. Of course, our language has a botanical word for such a structure, etaerio.

The question becomes: 'Can this etaerio structure be extended to non-technological words?' Which kernels can I place words like quango, gnarldom and glasnost with? If only I could find some answers, our language would become much neater.

I need help, so I publish an explanatory post on the Internet and ask for comments. The usual barrage of replies from smart-Alecs immediately gets dumped in the trash bin, leaving me to concentrate on the score of helpful e-mails from experts and academics. One from the Oxford English Dictionary goes: "Terrif idea. Why not authors as kernels? We've got letters from Jonathan Swift, Mary Shelley, Arthur Conan Doyle etc. Want to come and see? XX."

"XX?" I reply.

"Oops. Not kisses, honest. Name's

Xanthe Xena."

"Sounds like something from outer space."

"Had parents with a passion for ancient Greek. Lunch this Thursday? To talk about your working on our paper files."

Refusal is not an option. When I collect her from her office, she has, as I expect from the Xanthe part of her name, golden hair. What comes as a surprise is her air of belonging to world of proficient officialdom. Take away her glasses, let down her hair and replace her Oxford blue suit with a simple body-hugging dress, she is a super-model. A lady for all roles.

As etiquette demands, Xanthe bubbles and effervesces her way through trivia until coffee is served. She hands me a memory stick. "This contains our electronic files on definitions where authors have given their written permission for the public to see their emails. I've included those permissions in case you get any queries."

"That's very kind of you, but—"

"As for the pre-1986 slips and notebooks, they're papers of national importance over which we must take due care and diligence.

I'm required to ask you for references that you're a suitable person to be allowed access. Are you doing a doctorate, or have you published your results in an appropriate forum?"

Phew! Hypersonic efficiency always bamboozles me. I sip coffee while putting my thoughts in order. "I take it my post is insufficient?"

She nods. "We need some form of peer acceptance. I suspected you might be in this position, which is why I've included a file on the stick with list of accredited journals. The top three are those most likely to publish an article you could write based on your stance."

"Thank you. This is more than I could have ever expected. Can I ask what your interest is in all this?"

"Let's just say I'd like to see how you progress. That's all." She smiles demurely as if the business part of this meeting is over.

"I have a problem though."

"Oh?"

"I don't think I can use authors as kernels."

"Surely if they used the word first, then they deserve that right?"

"But did they? Take the word orc. Tolkien used it throughout his books and most people think he's its inventor. In reality, orc was defined by 1590 as a devouring monster, exactly as he used it. The same is true for his other words."

"Even hobbit?"

"Yes. It's derived from an Old English word, *holbytla* meaning hole-dweller. Obvious when you think about it."

"Interesting…" Xanthe stares at me as if I'm an alien.

I stare back at her still figure. Without warning a tress loosens from her perfect hairdo and quivers down onto her shoulder. She definitely has struck a chord with me. "You are a very attractive lady."

"Thank you." She smiles. "You're charming yourself."

Encouraged, I glance at her left hand. There's no wedding or engagement ring. "Dare I ask if you have a boyfriend?"

She raises her eyebrows without a wrinkle touching her forehead. "You certainly get straight to the point."

I give a brief nod.

"How can I put this?" She pauses. "My

life is less complicated without one."

I know my disappointment shows, but I can't help it. "I presume there's no chance of changing your mind?"

She shakes her head slowly.

I take a few seconds to stop my lips trembling from disappointment. "Maybe we could just be friends?" I hope this turns out to be a lie.

"Absolutely." She tucks her tress back into her hairdo with a flick of her fingers. "How are you going to group the rest of the words?"

"I don't know yet."

Going home, I feel as if I have missed a detail or two, an oddity that was out of place.

I spend the next weeks drafting my article. Xanthe promptly rewrites it into academese, which leads to a journal fast-tracking it into publication.

I revert to concentrating on the bigger issue. There is no obvious starting point for further analysis. In the absence of a better idea, I list the non-technical new words in order of first use. This needs access to the Dictionary's paper files to garner the exact date, which means regularly visiting the

Dictionary's office in Walton Street and seeing Xanthe.

One day after Xanthe brings out the file on Quisling, I ask: "Why is an intelligent lady like you working here as an ordinary assistant?"

She shrugs her shoulders. "I suppose I'm in love with English. It's the most complete language I know of."

"Wouldn't you be better off as a lecturer at the university?"

"I'm not that dry and dusty," she says going off in a huff.

To my surprise the list produces results. Political initiatives, new philosophies, and fashion and lifestyle fads cluster around obvious kernels. Yet, Xanthe's comment about completeness bothers me. What did she mean? Can other languages have concepts that English doesn't?

I discover that although rare, there are some examples. Russian has a word for the sovereign ownership of the seas. Swedish has one for the right to roam over the countryside. How can I link the English kernels to show up these gaps? Can I find more gaps?

Technology is not the area to explore. It

has already undergone intensive cross-fertilisation of ideas worldwide. Politics is far more promising.

I work my way from tribalism, through fiefdoms, kingdoms, empires, superpowers and federations, and on to regionalisation, to establish links between the political kernels. Throughout, territorial ownership is paramount. Space is different. It belongs to nobody and everyone at the same time. Yet no word exists to describe this specific paradox. I'm so excited by identifying my first gap in the English language that I hug and kiss Xanthe, much to the amusement of her colleagues.

How will politics change once we settle in space? How will we cope with xeno-politics if we meet aliens? Xen-what? Xen- a prefix meaning strange, foreign or a guest.

I stare at her as she works on her desk screen. She looks, feels and acts like a human. She has such a sense of humour and fun, even though I have never met anyone with a clearer and tidier mind. I'm in love with her, even now. Yes, her tresses fall astray without a jolt or pull, and not even the tiniest of wrinkles ever show on her face. Damn. Who am I kidding?

I spend the rest of the afternoon in shock, going through the motions of my research without really taking it in and thinking about the real societal set-ups in space. The cold hits as Xanthe and I leave the Dictionary's office that evening. While she locks up, I gaze at those few stars that shine through the streetlights' haze. "I wonder what kind of politics aliens have?"

"Why the deep thoughts?"

"Oh, it's just the stars move around. Any race owning one has continually changing boundaries. Just how do they work out who owns which bit of space?"

She laughs. "If there's nothing in that space, why worry about it?"

"On the contrary, sometimes it does matter. It only takes a star to get close enough for its gravity to pinch one of other star's planets…" I go silent to give her a chance to admit the truth.

She meets my silence with a deeper one.

"How would you get round it, Xanthe?"

She looks genuinely puzzled. "Maybe aliens find a way of keeping their planet or accept a payment from the other star's owners. Who knows? Who cares?"

"Both options would need a hefty amount of resource or energy. I don't think either would happen in reality."

"I don't know the answer then."

"I think you do."

"Why?'

"You're an alien."

"You're crazy."

"Am I? Apart from being rather aloof from the rest of us as if you're hiding something, your tresses aren't real hair, are they? And what about your lack of wrinkles which any lady would die for?"

"Then why would I put up with this job?" she says, nodding her head towards her office.

"Monitoring the progress of English. It's a good way of keeping track of our development as a species. Why English though? Don't tell me." I pause. "It's the most complete."

Seconds stretch out into minutes. "Nobody's going to believe you if you talk about me."

"I won't."

"What are you going to do?"

"Work out a fair system of territorial

rights for the stars. Then publish and push for it to be enacted in international law. Will that be enough for you aliens to visit us openly?"

"Perhaps. Where will you begin on this territorial system?"

"With what we've got now. A stellar etaerio with the stars as kernels."

"And then what?"

"Find and tie up the loose ends."

"I'd better keep my eye, or should I say an antenna on you."

I enjoy working on the problem. In fact, I'm addicted to making the galaxy, even the universe tidier. Some people might say Xanthe ensnared me, but it would be a strange kind of slavery as I can walk away from it anytime. I am, for the first time in my life, truly happy.

The First and Last Safe Place by C. John Arthur

Aleph felt his bones resonate. A storm approached.

He peered out over the parched ground where his buddies grazed. They could do with the rain, at least. He scratched his grey, thinning fur. His latest buddy sat on one shoulder. It was getting to such a size that it threw his balance as he edged across the ground. Most of his kind had a buddy pair, one on each shoulder of their rotund torsos.

Old age brought many hardships.

In the coming storm they needed to find safe places. He howled the warning cry. The others looked up from the withered vegetation. Rocky outcrops surrounded their grazing grounds; fissures in the rocks led to the wider plain outside. The rocks towered over them; grim black giants that offered protection from the storm. As the darkness grew, Aleph thought he could see a faint shaft of light in the centre of the plain. Perhaps it was the last rays of sunshine breaking through, but this strange illumination was always there just before the storm. The tribe saw it as an omen. There was much debate, however, whether it was a sign of doom or salvation.

They were aware, but avoided discussing, the fact that the storms were getting fiercer. And as their numbers grew, the number of safe places dwindled. Traditionally, they squeezed their rounded bodies into rocky alcoves; cavities scoured by the action of sand and wind.

With his warning cry the young scuttled and rolled into the alcoves, wedging their bodies in. The older, more mature individuals had been tunnelling; a new enterprise that had opened up in the last few cycles. By chance, their digging had exposed new bolt holes in the rock buried beneath the sandy plain. It was especially valuable for those whose buddies were maturing since the irregular shapes they found deep down accommodated their unevenly shaped bodies. It was here that Aleph needed to head. He hesitated as he heard a faint whisper in the wind, a sound shaped into his name.

The plain was deserted apart from the slow-moving buddies still heading towards the sheltering rocky outcrops. There was no obvious caller. He turned again to the mystic light. It appeared brighter than a few moments ago. There was speculation that it achieved its full strength at the height of the storm. But no living being had witnessed it. Such light might give hope, but it was insubstantial against the howling winds and the rocks that span effortlessly in a vortex, smashing all life to smithereens.

"Aleph."

His name again, called more clearly. The shaft of light flickered in time as if it was responsible.

Aleph shuddered. The siren call heard only by those close to death or deranged after being clubbed senseless by spinning rocks. He refused to look death in the face – surely he was not that old? And in any case, he had a buddy to protect. Madness was another thing, though. As his kind became old, madness was known. A madness that drove them out in the midst of the storm. If it was madness, why was it so personalized, why did it know his name?

He shrugged his compact body and ambulated towards a rocky outcrop where he recognized one of his old buddies was waiting for him, jittering up and down on her paws.

"Coming," he said, picking up the pace of his shuffles – rolling being out of the question with such a sizable buddy attached.

They entered a newly excavated tunnel. The buddy was pushing him from behind. In an instant, the ground they passed through could morph from a solid structure to a swirling cauldron of sand. The tunnel became steeper, but it was a struggle to keep moving. Aleph recognized the storm's intake of breath.

A vertical shaft opened in front of him and he plunged down, grabbing his buddy as he fell.

Their free-fall turned into a leisurely downward drift. They reached a tight constriction in the shaft and Aleph had to exhale to pass through.

Moments later their slow descent petered out. Aleph felt his body wobble and then they started to ascend, rapidly gaining momentum.

They returned the constriction in the shaft and Aleph sucked in a deep breath, wedging his body in place and holding on to his buddy firmly. The storm's eye must be upon them. The suction grew stronger. His buddy's grip bit into his hand, but he held on despite the pain. His whole arm wrenched in its socket, the buddy released their hold and shot upwards.

"No!" Aleph cried.

The upward force cut abruptly. He dropped like stone. On the way down outcrops of rock battered his body so that he was barely conscious when he hit the bottom.

*

Aleph came round; he was surrounded by several buddies. He ached all over.

"Peace, Aleph," an old buddy said, and the group around echoed the sound, so that the word peace gained a tune and then a harmony and finally a chorus that echoed through the tunnels. In that peace Aleph slept for many days.

Aleph awoke alone but found plants placed around him. He ate and returned to sleep.

Finally, several days later, his strength

returned, and he was relieved to find the new buddy on his shoulder was beginning to move – a very good sign after all he had endured.

Aleph requested that they go to the surface. The buddies looked at each other and made discouraging noises – but he insisted.

When they emerged, Aleph barely recognized the transition from the dark tunnels. Brooding purple clouds hid the sun. A shallow puddle covered much of their grazing ground. Many of the rocky parapets that once surrounded them had collapsed, casting enormous boulders out onto the plain. Aleph's spirit sank as he recognized there would be few survivors from the young who had wedged themselves into the traditional alcoves.

His attention was drawn to the shaft of light that had not faded but had remained steadfast in the middle of the plain. There was a slight tremor in his body, which he thought reflected the injury he had sustained. Then his whole torso throbbed.

Aleph shrieked a howl of despair.

A storm was returning, and after such a short break. They were lost.

His buddies were retreating back into the

tunnels, but Aleph doubted that they would find sanctuary even there. "Aleph!" they called. He felt the terror in their voices.

Aleph knew he and his new buddy would not survive a repeated battering, but at least he could offer comfort to his other buddies. He turned to follow them.

"Aleph."

Aleph's body twitched; it was the siren call again. He looked in the direction of the voice. The light was strangely attractive, and, at the end of his life, he found himself curious. The call had a warmth to it that only his parent had given him. Perhaps this was the madness that all reached in the end?

He shambled towards the shaft of light and as he passed into its beam, he felt the peace of ten thousand buddies singing in harmony. This was the place to die, to finally rest. He would watch his last storm from here. He imagined the end would be rapid.

*

The twisting black finger arrived. The light beam that Aleph stood in got brighter and solidified, so now Aleph sensed he was in a towering white cylinder.

A torrent of dark forces marched forward. Aleph realized the cloud that surrounded the dense vortex was not dust but fair-sized rocks, held in a wild dervish around the central core. The finger expanded and filled his vision. He could pick out individual slabs, any of which could have ended his life instantaneously. First one, then another collided with the shaft of light and bounced away. Smaller fragments blazed and then were no more.

Finally, Aleph understood he was in the only safe place.

The storm's roar reached a crescendo. Although Aleph was protected against the physical fury, the sound reverberated around his tired old body. He felt a peaceful warmth and settled gently down on the sandy ground.

*

Aleph awoke. There was a gentle light over her. She tugged her feet free from the soft anchor-point beneath her. She recognized her parent's empty corpse. The landscape was dramatically transformed, utterly distinct from the memories that came unbidden to her mind.

Smooth mounds of low rock surrounded her resting place. Of her kind, there was no trace.

Aleph remembered everything. And, more importantly, she knew with certainty the nature of the first and last safe place.

Lyonesses
by So Mayer

Ma Morvoren y'n Benbow	There's a mermaid in the Benbow
Deun alemma, voyd alemma	Let's go, let's get away
An tekka yw yn oll Kernow	The most beautiful in all of Cornwall
Kelmys on Ostrali.	We're bound for Australia.

— 'Deun Alemma'

They told us we'd never have the legs for it. That we'd be all over the pitch, hair getting in our faces, distracted by the dazzle and glare of the cameras and the fans, always trailing the opposition with tails between the sticks. Water carriers at best. And were we really women anyway?

We didn't listen. Stopped our ears with shoes, and ships, and sealing wax – except to the words of our coach, Dory.

Just keep swimming. Just keep swimming.

'Ma Morvoren y'n Benbow.

And sing. Sing when you're winning. We knew we could be irresistible.

*

We're not going to lie, sometimes it is like running on hot knives.

We've come late to legs, to this division between them, so the timing of a tackle can throw us off. Splashdown! Astroturf so much less forgiving than the ocean. Sometimes you just want the ground to swallow you up, but it doesn't, does it? It has no gulp, just bladed roughness. We all sport grazes, compare grass-cuts in the bath afterwards. The pattern that gravel makes on a knee is not unlike scales. We touch the tiny depressions, pour salt on the small wounds, feel grainy like we're breaking up. Get up and do it all again. Get knocked down and we get up again.

Just keep swimming, etc.

Don't call us divers, though. We know our opponents see us as easy targets, want to hack our legs from under us. Call them fake, then talk up our unfair advantage. Our unnatural body shape. Talk about cynical. But on the pitch, we bite our tongues, although then they call us dumb. Taunt us to sing, then, when they fall, call it cheating. When we fall, we stretch out each other's limbs, press them into the hum deep in our stomachs. We know where the cramp cramps in the new unfluid muscles as they try to swish and kink, powering us through sweaty air, around bodies as if coral.

Flick-on. It's on. We are still finding our feet, which gravity helps with. Anchoring; pointing This Way Up. Up and over, sometimes. We specialise in the bicycle kick, the flying finish. Our sweeper-keeper whose legs seem to move as one. The ball floating on the air like seafoam.

*

At exceptionally low spring tide, you can walk between the Scilly Isles. You can; we can. You even call the sound between St Mary's and Tresco The Road.

Lyonesse, the City on the Bottom of the Sea, has always been amphibious; both and everything else, too. Bedrock and birdrock and tombolo, outcroppings of the Cornubian batholith. Deep rock nearly three hundred million years old, so the stories go, told from seawitch to seawitch of the Great Uprising, aka what you call the Variscan orogeny: magma making mountains in the seams of Pangaea's coming-together. Stretching from Galicia to the Bohemian massif and down into Turkey, pivoted on Montblanc, it's the fold belt that holds Europe together, a stone spine mirrored across the Mediterranean by the Anti-Atlas; across the Atlantic by the Appalachians.

Deun alemma, voyd alemma.

To use your words, which we hear in the deep. Water is a transmitter, a medium of echoes and resonances. Your radar that causes cetaceans to go off course, tortured by songs they can't respond to; singers calling to them of nowhere, out of nowhere. You have become what you fear of us, the fatal voice luring the world onto the rocks. Rocks you give names to, names that hiss and sizzle in our sea-ears, rocks you do not understand. We have grown on them like barnacles; grown with them. The seawitches say we too, in our first forms, swam forth as the Earth's crust extended, carried in the tides of granitic magma.

Hot knives, cooled to 1000° celsius. Fractures form along vertical joints. It is all one to us, and of us: under and over, hidden and exposed. Where we rub along the waves, where we come to the surface. Either way, we erode. Those fantastic shapes you call tors our stopped bodies playing keepy-uppy, scattered about with the irreducible core of us, rounded and hard, to be navigated with care. What you call clitter. Bearded with ferns and lichens, mossy boulders all clustered and jumbled together, warm beneath you on a summer's day. Over here the clitter of Lustleigh Cleave, just below Harton Chest.

Be still my...

What we mean is: this land is us, magma-veined and weighty, cool enough to stand tall even if we crack slowly under pressure. We are the foot of the country dipped in between the English Channel and the Celtic Sea, toe pointed balletically, Ireland flying off our laces into the Atlantic's wide-open net. GOAAAALLLLLL.

How could we miss?

*

St. Blazey AFC, across the river from Par, was the first place we walked onto pitch. Maybe the team's name made us think of those undersea fires that forged us, or it was the draw of Lostwithiel called to us, sang of the Lost City Beneath the Waves. Maybe it was just the club's gas-heated showers. The Par river runs alongside the pitch, down to St Austell Bay. We came around the Lizard heading north-east, ears ringing with the busy shipping lanes going south from Plymouth. Up into Carlyon Bay. Car-Lyon. Here we are, already. Here we go, here we go, here we go.

An tekka yw yn oll Kernow

Summer of 2019, mostly cool and wet, like us. Late, late June aglitter of a sudden and we're drawn up like a tide by the sounds of it,

#FIFAWWC, the talk of the beaches and boats, the news of it crackling through submarine cables running from Sennen Cove and Porthcurno, Bude and Skewjack, across the Atlantic in thick skeins ablaze with the chatter. It had pricked our ears for the first time in 2015, voices going back and forth across the ocean, rising data usage, viewing figures, intensities. Four years on and it's coming home coming home; so-called. Not to Kernow, there's no Cornubians among the Lionesses. Bring back my bonny to me.

We made our fantasy first XI: our queen and hero Pinoe, who tells the press "You can't win without gay players," playing for pride; seagreen-haired Gaëlle Enganamouit, Marta of the flaming lips, Wendie Renard rising above every challenge, Vanina Correa keeping the Albiceleste shining, Kadeisha Buchanan magical youngest of seven sisters, Kim Little the legend of Mintlaw, Yuka Momiki who wrote her thesis on the women's game, @rasheedatt10 sharing the Super Falcons' R&R on Insta, Lucy Bronze moving fluid as hot metal strong as a statue. Phew. We argued their stats and their merits as we practised; we were – we are – all muscle, one long curving kick, used to the rough-and-tumble of the world's worsening weather all summer storm and hurricane, but getting something *into* a net we had to get used to.

Up until that day we sauntered up the Par in our glittering kits, stitched bluegreen out of algae, St. Blazey had never had a women's team. Despite being one of the oldest clubs in the county (founded 1896), they had no place in the Electrical Earthbound Cornwall Women's Football League. We must have seemed an unlikely fit, being neither eels nor, exactly, earthbound. But at level 7 (seabed, bedrock, bottom feeders) who's to argue? Helston, Charlestown, Penryn, Illogan, Mousehole, Bude, FXU, RNAS Culdrose, Newquay Celtic, Porthleven, Wadebridge all fell before us in the 2019/20 season, and so too the other Saints (Agnes whose hair grew and covered her body, Breward bishop of Jersey, Teath daughter of Brycheiniog and companion of Breaca), and lo! we were promoted to the South West Women's Football League Division One (West). To the South West Premiere League. The FA Women's National League South, the Championship, the Women's Super League.

Sing and keep singing.

Having climbed out of the sea, we kept climbing. Cliffs of fall and get up again. Just keep swimming. We split our training between exposed rock and our secret grounds undersea. Did high-intensity training in the photosynthesis chamber at the Eden Project, swimming high as kites in plant-exhaled oxygen behind the glass. Kept our selkie skins in the club dressing rooms, kept moist by those gas-heated showers. Down the river and into the salt, our metamorphic world. Under pressure.

*

We swam to and from WSL games as much as we could; swam round the south coast, risking all those shipping lanes and daytripping ferries, to meet Bristol, then on to Brighton & Hove, where we shimmied up the pier to celebrate a 3-0 victory. Swam east to sneak in a friendly with Equality FC at the Dripping Pan, £5 gate and kids in free, played out in the pouring autumn rain. Later in the season we suffered the New River Canal to play Arsenal (goalless draw, we were all sick as parrots from the parasites in the water), the weekend saved by a knock-up with Goaldiggers and Lush Lyfe FC raising funds with Playing for Kicks. Thousands in funds thanks to a tweet from *The Last Leg*.

The Grand Union Canal was a grander way to playing Birmingham at Solihull Moors; with lightly-wrinkled fingers we leafed locally through Alys Fowler's *Hidden Nature* in the dressing room, charting her coracle course with our waterborne senses, charmed by her herons and blue-purple buddleia, her girlfriend and her oars. Plain water – calling it fresh is a stretch – is not our way but we will take it; not to our taste but we can breathe it, briefly. We are never without a crisp packet, the snap and crackle (how we miss the deep blue taste of Smiths salt n shake). We map post-match chippies to keep our lithium in balance, our lithic electrolytes. Don't drink from our water bottles pitch-side; too saline for you, emetic.

St Blaise, patron saint of St Blazey and one of the Fourteen Holy Helpers, is known for healing illnesses of the throat. He stopped a child choking on a fishbone at his feet, even as he was being taken into custody by

Agricola, the governor of Cappadocia and Armenia, on the orders of the emperor Licinus. Agricola had him beaten and skinned with iron combs, then beheaded.

We know how he feels.

Everywhere we go, they throw combs at us, a taunt at our vanity or our fragility. In the hopes they will catch in our shoulder-length, waist-length, knee-length, ankle-length hair, trip us up, discombobulate us into bobbing the ripple of it. Is it OK? For so long, every away dressing room, they covered the mirrors superstitiously, as if that will disconnect us from the sea, as if it would make us disappear. They covered the toilet bowls with clingfilm. Slip in cameras and mirrors to find out how we pee. Please. We are magma, hot enough to melt plastic. To fuse glass. We have made ourselves who we are, not part-this and part-that, but all. All.

We shrug it off like our sealskins. Like water off a seal's back. Like we're impervious. Like you believe that. But keep making martyrs of us, and we will still keep winning.

*

We heard about it because of Barawa 2018, played in London as the base of the Somali diaspora. Only hints, whispers of CONIFA. Cornwall joined that same year (the same year also of the first CONIFA women's match, Kibris Türk FF vs. FA Sápmi, played in Northern Cyprus), confederate of independent football associations. Ellan Vannin (original hosts of the CONIFA European Cup 2015, placing third when it was played in Székely Land; semi-finalists at the inaugural 2014 Sápmi CONIFA World Cup after a dramatic penalty shoot-out against Kurdistan), Parishes of Jersey and Yorkshire were already members from these islands. We petitioned the Kernow Football Alliance to recognise us as the county team, Women's Super League runners-up 2027; to send us as Cornwall to the 2029 CONIFA World Cup, the first to feature a women's tournament.

"We say 'tell us what your identity is, and let's help you represent that through football.'" Paul Watson, CONIFA's head of member development.

CONIFA. For all our domestic success, it has become our obsession, a way out of

Brexissues about European cup football, transfers, even county lines. This is not who we are: we are freedom of movement. We are a refuge from warming seas. We sing, as we have long sung, in the Atlantic tongues of Gaelic and Brythonic and Tamazight and Tashelhiyt, the ancient sweet sounds of Judeo-Berber from the Moroccan coast; in the Mediterranean sounds of Sard and lenga d'òc provençau, Galego and Malti and Arabic. Your words, our words. On the pitch we shout in Sabir, the sailors' lingua franca of the millennial Med, heavy with Geonese, Venetian, Catalan and Berber; excellent for swearing, undetected, one seaborne element of Polari, the definitive proof of the Sabir-Wharf hypothesis that sailors are the structural basis of all *lingua franca*. Our fans chant:

Se ti sabir
Ti respondir
Se non sabir
Tazir, tazir

If you know / Then reply / If you don't / Be quiet.

*

Meet Kelly Lindsay, CONIFA Director of Women's Football. We pasted pictures of her USA career all around the St Blazey dressing rooms, adorning her portrait with shells and seaglass. We cheered on the Afghanistan women's football team she managed to victory at their second Central Asian Women's championships in 2023, after FIFA stripped the country's football federation of oversight of the women's team they had sexually, physically and legally abused. Captain Shabnam Mobarez and Mina Ahmadi were our outspoken heroes; even more after we heard that Mobarez, alongside players from twenty different countries, set a new world record for the lowest altitude match ever played, by the Dead Sea in Jordan. What salt she showed.

We once swam the bitter waves of the North Sea to Aalborg to see Mobarez play at home, making landfall, where else, at Klitmøller, before rounding the Jammerbugt over Skagen. Yes, and after that game, we did swim south through the waters of Kattegat, past Elsinore along the Orësund Strait, to see her, the one you always ask us about, at the Langelinie pier: still on her rock despite being blown up once and decapitated thrice.

May St. Blaise bless her and keep her. She had no comb to defend herself, only a rope of seaweed; maybe – maybe – her sealskin in disguise.

Yes, she is our sister. He stole her, the one who put her in a book; the one who put her in a ballet; the one who turned her into bronze with the profits from his father's beer. All of them, and only one of her (and yet thirteen licensed copies of the statue around the world). In 2029, the very same year as the first CONIFA Women's World Cup, the copyright expires, and we will bring her – all of her – back where she belongs.

In the story, Andersen the sad sadist curses her – this cut-off part of himself, iron comb for his own back, his own internalised homophobia – to three hundred years as seafoam-become-spirit (albeit electrically earthbound; bound to do good deeds for the men who betrayed her). The statue has had seventy years.

It's coming home.

*

When we go to play in Sápmi next year – and we will – she will be with us, on the team, our talismanic number 9. There's no net she can't shred; no challenge in the air she can't win. But don't call her Ariel, that other lie naming her for the element she was dissolved into, residue of Andersen's self-pitying tears.

We swim in them, sea temperatures rising with all your human sad sadism, punishing yourselves to breathe carbon monoxide, to eat lead, to piss plastic oestrogen. We take it all in through our gills, have learned to excrete it deep undersea, into vents already toxic with sulphur. Who knows what new species will rise to the surface as the Scillies finally drown. No more Road. It is always high tide. This time, when we swim north, it will be in temperate waters filled with basking sharks and swimming crabs and blackbelly rosefish and splendid alfonsino and tiny horse mackerel following their food Calanus helgolandicus come north from Heligoland. In Sápmi, in Staare, we will meet teams from other drowned islands and cities, from scorched places and refugee nations. At Mid Sweden University they will talk as well as play. We, of the sea, have to be there.

Kelmys on Ostrali.

If we can't play for Kernow, who now narrow-sightedly demand Cornish-born players only, we'll play for the sea, which knows no country. Our identity is insurgent as magma, granite-strong, stretching across the globe. Help us represent, CONIFA. Bring together our saline sorority; permit us our Permian sisterhood of the Variscan: Moroccan, Iberian, Sardinian, Celtic. We've been cast as statues and silenced; cast as villainous seducers and chastised. Shamed for our tails; told to jam them between our legs, which are called false because we made them for ourselves. Illusions, confusions; enhancements we haven't earned. Punishments we've brought on ourselves. Penalties, either way.

Sing when you're winning, they taunt us.

Ask the sunken lands of Lyonesse. The sea always wins.

The Lego Calf by Jon Bilbao

Please let me start by apologising for sending you this letter, since we have never met. I had initially thought of coming to your house and telling you in person what I am going to write here, but then I thought this would be a better way to do things: it puts us both in a much less awkward position and it allows me to choose my words better. In any case, I trust you will forgive me my likely hesitations.
Once you have finished reading this letter and have thought about what I have written, should you feel that you want to take this further, please do not hesitate to call me on the number I have included at the end of this letter.
And now allow me to apologise again, this time for starting my story with something so painful as my wife's illness and death. I have no idea whether you and Sara knew each

other. You may well have bumped into each other when dropping off the children or picking them up from school, I don't know. As long as her health allowed, Sara would always take care of those duties. If you did in fact know each other and she ever mentioned you to me, I cannot remember now.

She had suffered no noticeable discomfort or symptoms until a routine gynaecological examination diagnosed her condition. By then the cancer had spread so far that it was a wonder Sara felt so well. However, from that moment on, things went downhill very quickly. Sara had to quit her job and focus on her recovery. Well, we called it recovery; the doctors called it treatment, a much less compromising term.

We didn't hide the truth from our son, although we didn't reveal quite how serious it was. He is ten - old enough to realise that something was wrong. Soon it was impossible to hide Sara's physical decline and she couldn't pay him as much attention as before. Shortly after that, she could barely pay him any attention at all. I took time off work to look after her and to spend as much time together as possible.

I also took care of our son, to the extent that I could manage to find the motivation and the energy. During the early days this was no great challenge. He has always been a quiet and introverted child, easily engrossed in his own fantasy world. He loves reading and drawing. He can spend hours in his room, happy to entertain himself without any need for company.

I would devote a bit of each evening with him in his bedroom. I wanted him to know that we were concerned about him despite what was happening. I asked him about school. To tell you the truth, it wasn't all that easy to talk with him. In fact, it was impossible to get him to say two sentences in a row. Before long, neither of us knew what to say, so we would sit in silence. I would try to find excuses to remain in his room, but it must have been obvious that I wanted to leave, and I'm pretty sure he preferred to be on his own.

When I was a kid, I loved building things, and I still do… Actually, not so much now.
One day, as I returned from the chemist's, I stopped at a toy shop and bought my son a Lego set. It contained all the pieces for building a tipper truck.
He received this gift poker-faced, which is his usual way. He opened the box on his table and just stared at the pieces as though he had no idea what to do with them. I suggested building the truck together and, fearing he would say no, I got started right away without waiting for an answer. I did most of the work, though I explained each step along the way using the illustrated instructions. It was a nice truck - the back tipped up to unload. I went to the kitchen and filled it up with rice as if the truck were carrying a load of gravel. I asked my son if he liked this, and he said he did.
The following day, when I went into his room, the Lego truck was still on the table even though it had been pushed to one side. I asked him if he wanted us to build something else; the instructions suggested a couple of less

impressive alternatives that you could build from the same pieces. I had to insist to get him to agree. We took the truck apart and chose one of the other options. This time he was more participative - in fact, he did most of the work while I read out the instructions.

And so, we got into the habit of building things together. I bought him one or two Lego kits every week. We would chat as we fitted the pieces together, though not a lot. After the tipper we made other building industry items: a steamroller, a crane, an excavator… Next, we moved on to Lego Architecture sets. In a model shop in the town centre I found Frank Lloyd Wright's Fallingwater house set, then the Guggenheim in New York, and the Empire State Building. I came to look forward to those times we spent together.

One afternoon I walked into his room and, to my surprise, I saw he was building something on his own. I would usually have had to ask him more than once to stop what he was doing so that we could start playing with the Lego. But that afternoon he had placed all the pieces from all the sets I had given him into a pile and was building something that I couldn't identify. He was working without instructions and was so focused that he didn't even notice me. I thought it best not to disturb him. That day Sara was suffering more than usual, so I went off to stay by her side.

Sara's condition worsened with each day that passed, so I hardly had a chance to be with the boy, who stayed in his room almost all the time he was at home. On the few occasions I popped in, I noticed that he was still involved in his building project. The thing he was building looked unlike anything I had ever seen, just a meaningless jumble of pieces, a kind of tower with an apparently random series of protrusions sprouting from it. The mixture of colours of the pieces, assembled in no apparent pattern, made the whole thing even more disconcerting and ugly.

Sara became so ill that she had to be hospitalised. My mother came round to take care of the kid. I hardly saw him at all, I was so focused on keeping Sara company.

My wife died a week later.
Even if it were essential for the purposes of this letter to describe the few days that followed, I don't think I could bring myself to recall the details.
All that time, the thing my son had built had stayed on the table in his room. It would have been impossible not to notice it, standing half a metre high and just as wide, more or less spherical in shape, and solid-looking.
To tell you the truth, I didn't pay it much attention. For me, our Lego building days were relegated to the distant past, like so much else. I assumed he thought the same way and that the only reason he had kept it there was that he couldn't be bothered to take apart all the many pieces that made it up.
I went back to work. I had to keep myself busy. Meanwhile, my son was becoming more and more introverted, and although I could see it happening, I was powerless to do anything about it. I would pop into his room and sit next to him and we would exchange a few words. I would stroke his head like someone

reluctantly rubbing a lamp found in the attic, vainly hoping a genie would come out.
I am not trying to excuse myself here.
With things as they were, you will understand my joy when I came home one day to find him playing with another kid from his school. My son hadn't been so happy in weeks. The two of them were busy adding new pieces to the Lego construction. I didn't ask where they had got them from. I could hear them whispering excitedly from the hallway.
The next day my son was playing alone again. When I asked him about his friend, he told me that he had a karate class that afternoon. A few days later, when I asked him the same question, he just shrugged. I decided to leave it at that.
However, not long after that, another classmate came round to play. They too played with the Lego construction. This new friend added some pieces that he took out of a crumpled supermarket bag. He obediently placed them wherever my son told him to. Just like the previous kid, this one came to our

house only once. He added the pieces he had brought, and I never saw him again.

There were more visits like that one, just as fleeting. All the children brought pieces of Lego - some with whole boxfuls, others with hardly a handful, stuffed in their pockets.

I asked him how they would sort out whose pieces were whose when they took the thing apart. My son stared at me as if this hadn't occurred to him but said it wouldn't be a problem. I also asked him what they were making, and he said he wasn't sure. Were they planning to find out how far they could get by adding more and more pieces? Yes, he said, that was the plan.

Some days later, I went into my son's room while he was out the house. I needed a pen and I thought I might find one among his things.

The Lego construction now filled the whole table and already stood over a metre high. I must admit that it was impressive. I bumped into it while searching in his drawers - it would have been difficult not to. There were a

great many arms sticking out of it, some of which protruded beyond the edge of the table. It was one of these upper arms, which were the most recent additions to the construction, that I had knocked into. The arm broke off and fell onto the floor. I quickly picked it up, but before I could fix it back on again, something caught my eye.
Several pieces had also come loose from the area where the arm connected to the construction, revealing a hollow space, scarcely bigger than a matchbox, inside that thing. There was something in there. I had to take a few more pieces apart to get it out. It was a piece of paper, folded over and over again. I unfolded what looked like a page ripped out of a notebook. At the top of the page I read: "I want a new watch." Below it was a drawing of a digital watch with various buttons. The writing was childish, and the drawing had been done with wax crayons. The request was underlined several times and the author had drawn shining rays emanating from the words and the watch.

The writing was not my son's, and neither was the drawing – he draws much better. I assumed that the author was one of the children who had recently come round to the house.
Carefully I detached more parts of the assembly in search of more inner chambers. I found two, containing doubly folded wishes: "I want to be taller" and "I want not to be laughed at." Both requests were accompanied by their corresponding drawing. In the first was a stick person with very long legs; in the second, another effigy, this time with broad shoulders and disproportionately large fists and at his feet were other, ant-sized figures. Again, both had the same shining yellow and orange rays emanating from both words and pictures. The handwriting was different in each one and was also different from the first paper. None of them were my son's.
I took it for a childish game. We used to make things like that too when I was a kid, in fact it was mostly the girls. They would write requests and put them in boxes or bottles

which they would bury among the roots of a tree.

I preferred not to look any further, afraid that I would not be able to reassemble the thing. I slipped the notes back into their secret chambers and re-assembled the pieces I had removed.

In the weeks that followed, every time a kid came home with a new offering of Lego pieces and a folded slip of paper in his pocket, I would amuse myself guessing what he would ask for. Not to have to wear glasses? For his parents to buy him cooler clothes? To have smaller ears?

When my son was out the house, I would take apart the latest additions to the construction and look for the requests. Sometimes they coincided with what I had imagined. Other times they did not: "I want to see any women I want naked", "I want people not to speak so loud".

In any case, they were always just kids' stuff. I wasn't worried.

However, I did start to worry when a kid came round who didn't just add new pieces and then disappear but kept coming round again and again. I would find him there almost every day. He always brought new Lego pieces as his offering. He was tall for his age, silent and polite. I was not at all surprised that he and my son got on so well together.

Just in case you were wondering: that boy was your son and the reason why I am writing this letter.

It was several days before I had the chance to go back into the boy's room, dismantle part of the construction and read the new requests. There was only one. I assumed it had been put there by your son.

The message on the paper said: "I want my parents to die." The drawing perfectly illustrated those words: two dismembered bodies, limbs and heads separated from the torsos, abundant blood and the usual rays of power shining out from it all. An explanatory note stated "Mum" next to the head with long hair, and "Dad" next to the other one.

Now you will understand why I decided to write you this letter instead of meeting and talking face to face. Had I done that, once I reached this point in the story, you would most likely have been shocked and incredulous and told me to shut up. You would have thrown me out of your house without waiting to hear a word more, and understandably so. At best, you would have demanded explanations that I could not possibly provide. As it is, you might still be so indignant as to stop reading, and perhaps even screw up these pages unread and toss them into the waste bin. Yet on the other hand – and I sincerely hope this will be the case – later, when your anger has died down, your curiosity might let you read until the end of my story.

That very night, after dinner, I went to talk to my son and told him how I'd noticed one boy coming to our house a lot and I asked who he was. The usual reply: just a classmate. In fact, he added, they weren't really mates, they just played together. I asked him if he had ever been to his classmate's house and he said no. As we talked, he was leafing through a comic. He would pause before he replied, as if he needed time to think about what to say next, or maybe he had simply lost interest in our conversation. I persisted: even if he hadn't been to that boy's house, surely he knew the parents? Apparently not. I asked him if his playmate ever talked about them. Either he didn't or my son didn't remember. I asked him if he had ever seen them. This time the answer was yes - he had seen them several times, when they came to pick up their son from school; sometimes the father, other times the mother. I asked him what they were like. My son shrugged and just said they were normal.

I stood mulling over his answer. He carried on reading his comic. I was getting more and more angry and annoyed with that story. He must have noticed this, because I caught him glancing at me and then he got up as if to leave the room. I ordered him not to move. I asked him again what it was that they were building and he replied the same as before - he didn't know what it was, just a game of sticking more and more pieces together. Then I asked him, scarcely hiding my irritation, how long this game would be going on for. He looked at me confused - apparently he didn't know. I asked him how he would know when it was over? How would he know when it was time to stop adding more pieces? I told him I wanted a specific answer, but he just stared at me in silence. Then I told him that I didn't like his game, that I was fed up with that thing, and I ordered him to take it apart. He complained and tried to stall. He asked me if he couldn't just leave it there a little longer. I asked how much longer and what for. Just a few more days, he said.

Of course, my answer was no. I told him to start taking it apart right then and there.

He shut himself in his room. After a while I went to tell him that it was bedtime. I found him sitting at the table with a piece of Lego in his hand. He was singing softly, lost in contemplation. He had taken apart two of the extremities and part of a third. The central area that held the requests remained intact. When I complained that he'd only done this much, he replied that it was more difficult than it appeared. Some bits were glued together and it was really difficult to pull them apart. I ordered him to brush his teeth and get off to bed.

The next morning, I called work to say I would be late. I waited until the kid had gone to school and went into his room. I would take it apart myself.

It took much longer than I had anticipated. It was true that some pieces seemed to be welded together. I saved each request that I found so that I could throw them all away later. The pieces were building up into a pile on the carpet in the middle of the room.

At last I reached the lower level, made up of the Lego that I had bought him. It was then that I found a new piece of paper, one that I had not seen before. This time it was my son's handwriting. His request was this: "I want my mother to just get on and fucking die." I prefer not to describe the drawing that accompanied these words. As I said, my son draws extremely well.

That very first request was buried under a mass of pieces that other kids had brought. I read it several times, then I put it away and finished taking the construction apart. Actually, I threw it against the wall again and again until it smashed to pieces.

I threw away all the requests, except for my son's. Now I realise that I should have kept yours too, but I hope you will take my word for it.

When my son got back from school that afternoon, I was waiting for him. I let him go into his room first, then followed him in a moment later. My son was standing in the doorway staring at the pile of Lego rising from the carpet. I told him that I had saved him the bother of taking it apart. Contrary to what I expected, he seemed totally unfazed. I asked him if he minded that I had done it myself and he muttered that he didn't. Then he asked me if that was all, as he pointed at

the pieces. I said of course that was all. What else could there be? He stared at me and repeated the question. I replied that the pile contained everything that had been in the construction. Nothing was missing. He looked thoughtfully back at the pieces and nodded. He said he would clear them away later.
Why should he be upset? I had not destroyed anything important, a mere image of the thing to which he and the other children, including your son, had dedicated their requests. My action had the same effect as tearing up an image of the Virgin Mary.
You will now understand why I need to tell you all of this, because I am quite sure that neither you nor your husband deserves what your son wishes for you, just like Sara didn't deserve that. Because you are normal, just like she was, and I am.

Bilbao, November 2010

Time Keep
by Elad Haber

There is a tiny town at the tip of time. Think of time as a pyramid. At the bottom are the ancient eras of dinosaurs, massive oceans, and century long winters. As the pyramid narrows, the eras are shorter and busier with life. And balanced at the top is a town full of tiny people. Though the town has no official designation, you may call it Time Keep.

The Keep's mayor, a bulbous man, well-coiffed and dressed primarily in navy blue, is named Mr. Sturges. Eternally a bachelor, he lives in the top-most floor of City Hall. Every morning, he drinks his tea and stares out the circular window to the town square and the clock tower that serves as a replacement sun. The face of the clock is shaped like a pyramid.

The past few decades have been very busy in the town. Once every generation, the pyramid is flipped, and time resets itself. Floods and massive storms blanket the planet called Earth, which is the single purvey of the Keep. The clock is rewound, and time starts anew. Time moves differently in the Keep so one generation up here accounts for thousands of years below.

The Mayor rises from his chair and picks up his pocket watch. It is a gold-plated disc with the names of all previous mayors etched into it. His father's name is the last on the list and then his grandfather and so on through his ancestry. Sturges has no children. When his time in office is up, the townsfolk will hold their first election in centuries.

Or so they think.

He descends the spiral staircase to the third floor of City Hall where his assistant hands him a type-written schedule for the day. Her name is Mrs. Point, a bookish be-speckled woman in a beige dress.

The mayor peruses the schedule. It has the usual meetings with Management. It has an hour-long block of time in grey with no label or description. Sturges smiles at Mrs. Point, folds the paper schedule neatly into his pocket, and proceeds downstairs.

The rest of the morning is dull, as usual. Sturges half-listens to petitioners with minor grievances and cabinet members with their endless agendas. His mind wanders to the grey area of his schedule. He stands up and checks his pocket watch.

"I need to go," he announces, "or I'll be late." There is some protest, but it is half-hearted.

Mrs. Point is waiting for him at the large wooden door downstairs. Sturges puts on his coat, a slightly darker shade of his signature blue, his bowler hat, and grips his favorite walking stick. He thanks her then steps out into the morning. The Keep has no sun or moon or day or night, yet the town was built to mirror the Earth below, so it has morning time and night time and the sky lightens and darkens through some trickery. He's never been quite sure of the specifics, except that it works.

He steps onto the cobblestone streets of the town square. He stops at a few of the open-air carts, businessmen and women selling fruit and other perishables, and chats with them while they offer him gratis goods. Every passerby nods at him.

The townsfolk are, for the most part, hard-working stalwarts of the way things have always been. They don't question their work, deep in the bowels of the town with the large gears and the heavy machinery of time. But there are others who spend hours sitting at the edges, gazing below to follow the brief lives of the Earth people.

It takes him a long while to wind his way out of the square. He enters a deserted alley and then surveys the street. When he's satisfied that he's out of view, he ducks into a vestibule and to a small door, half concealed behind a garbage bin. He knocks three times.

A small, dirty, man opens the door. The superintendent of the building is a short and fat fellow. They always are. He leads the mayor without a word through his darkened apartment and to a dingy elevator.

He's already excited. This is the part he loves the most. The clandestine maneuvers, the danger of being caught, exposed. There's a noise from down the hall. He freezes as if that would make him invisible. When the noise dies down, he continues to the furthest door down the hall and knocks once.

The dark-haired woman who opens the door is naked. She's been waiting. He grabs her waist as he shoves the door closed behind him, much louder than he should have. He feels that danger reverberate through his chest and down to his hard genitals. His breathe is already coming out short and tight. He pulls the woman, whose name he can never remember (Linda? Beverly?), to a nearby couch and unzips his pants.

It's quick but satisfying.

*

Below the streets and the shops and the buildings of the town are the Gears. There are no days off and no vacations. Time never stops.

One of the most seasoned veterans of the Gears is a slender and tall man named Mr. Benjamin Benedict. In the cavern that marks the entrance, tired workers, their clothes and skin caked in soot, nap between shifts on the muddy ground. In the rafters above the entrance are the latest examples made by Management. The shapes barely resemble that of bodies. They were hung there and starved to death.

Benedict tries not to look up at the hanging forms. He follows the phalanx of people as they move closer together into the tight halls and dark passageways of the Gears. Wood planks cover the rock below. Steam shoots out from cracks in the walls and crevasses in the ground. Lanterns hang from the ceilings and sway with the occasional wind. Men shout to be heard over the clatter.

He can start to hear the great force of the Gears while still on the elevator. He pulls two bright orange plugs out of his pocket and shoves them into his ears, making sure they are as far in as possible. The elevator continues its slow descent. The glow of the gold gears replaces the darkness of the topmost levels. Finally, the elevator stops and Benedict steps onto the metal passageways.

He's worked here on Gold level for the past decade in a managerial position. Most of his day-to-day work involves scheduling shifts, but his passion is in the measurements and calculations of time. He's not considered Management; those people don't work in the Gears. They work in comfortable offices aboveground with their shades drawn. Ben files reports to them once a week though he doubts they are ever read.

He begins his usual walk around the

various hanging platforms above the gears when rough hands grab him by the shirt and shove him into shadow.

"Hey!" he shouts. A hand grips his mouth to shut him up. He spins around to face his attacker only to see his brother, Charles.

"No time to explain!" Charlie shouts into his ear. He grabs Ben's arm and leads him down the hall and to a door he has never been in before.

Charlie ushers him into the dark room and shuts the door. The ever-present sound of the gears is muffled back here so they can talk without shouting.

"What is going on?" Ben demands.

Charlie is breathing heavy as if he's been running. They used to be mistaken for twins. He's shorter than Ben but has the same lanky build and hair color. Ben keeps his sandy brown hair tightly cropped, Charlie wears it long and loose. Ben never married, Charlie has a wife and two sons.

Charlie rummages around in the darkness for a moment. A lantern clicks to life and Charlie holds it up, illuminating the room.

In the center of the small room a rotund man is strapped to a chair. His arms and legs are tied with silver tape and his head is obscured by a hood, loose enough so that he can breathe. Ben recognizes the Mayor's distinctive form. Aghast, he looks at his brother.

"I screwed up," Charlie admits.

*

The hood is made of a dry stringy material that keeps getting stuck in the mayor's mouth. He's tried to cough it out, but that's only made it worse.

Sturges can hear men whispering in the room. He knows they're in the Gears, in one of the deep levels. He can hear the constant churning and feel the reverberations in his chest.

Everything had happened so fast. After his brief but exciting liaison, he descended the elevator, still a bit out of breath. The basement apartment was darker than he remembered but he still walked in like a fool. The men (or maybe it was just one) came at him from behind with a club or a hammer. He hit the ground hard and blacked out. When he came to, he was being dragged through the Gears.

He knows he has to try something. Despite the wooly texture filling his mouth, he tries to speak.

"Hello friends," he says from the inside of the hood. "If I may say something?"

A pause in the whispering. Sturges takes this as good sign and speaks up.

"Things have obviously gotten out of control here. Let's talk. Face to, uh, face. I promise not to rush to judgment or anger. We can make a deal, right?"

Struges smiles underneath the hood, hoping his conciliatory mood would be infectious. There's silence for a moment and then the sound of a door closing.

*

Above, news of the Mayor's disappearance has trickled out to the population. Citizens have gathered in the town square. Normally this is the time the square empties out, all the carts are wheeled aside, and only young lovers and old couples stroll hand-in-hand, welcoming in the evening. Tonight, there is a bevy of activity in City Hall. People rush in and out and whenever the wooden door opens, everyone tries to get a glimpse of what's going on inside.

The black suits of Management appear from one of the nearby buildings and stand like a lone black cloud away from the mass of people. They don't enter City Hall. They don't usually interfere with inter-town politics or goings on. Their focus is on Time. Still, the disappearance has obviously slowed work in the Gears otherwise they wouldn't have bothered to show up.

As the sky darkens, more people fill the square. Some of the clever cart owners start selling food and drink. There's an almost party-like atmosphere.

Finally, after the streetlights have been lit and the children escorted home, the large wooden door of City Hall opens. The Constable, a stern barrel-chested man with a thick mustache that shudders when he speaks, emerges. The murmuring of the townsfolk quiets. The Constable balls his fists and proclaims:

"We will hunt down whoever is responsible for this kidnapping!" His voice rises. "And we will make them pay!"

*

Ben and Charlie stand in a conspiratorial huddle outside the room.

Charlie has his hands up in a pleading gesture. "Ben, he was fucking my wife! I had to do something."

Ben shakes his head. "They'll hang you for this." He turns to walk away. "I'm not getting involved."

"Wait. Slow down!" Charlie grabs his brother's shoulder. "Maybe there's a way we can use this to our advantage? I know I was stupid, and I made a rash decision, but maybe we can use this for the cause. We can—"

"Keep your voice down!"

Charlie tries to keep his voice to a whisper just above the ever-present sound of the Gears. "Ben, we've been waiting for something like this."

"No!" Ben is rarely angry. "We can't be rash or quick to action. Not this time."

Charlie grits his teeth. The heavy sound of multiple footsteps comes from down the hall. The brothers share a frightened look.

This time, it's Ben who grabs his brother by the shoulders and whispers in his ear,

"Go!" he commands. "Hide! I'll hold them off." He speaks fast, his mind racing. "When they're gone, go to my office. Under my desk is a hidden panel. You'll find a plan in there. Now go!"

With all his might, Ben shoves Charlie into the shadows.

The Constable's men rush into the hall and grab Ben before he can protest. They push him up against a wall. They open the unmarked door and when they see the bound form of the Mayor, they smile. Then their smiles turn dark, and they set upon Ben, punching and kicking him until he goes limp.

Two of the deputies carry Ben back towards the elevators while the remaining ones untie the Mayor, apologizing all the while.

*

It's an event.

Morning in the Keep is usually filled with the steady march of worker's feet and the humdrum sounds of merchants setting up shop. Today, after a restless night for most of the population, the only sound is the rhythmic beating of a single tool in the town square.

A man is building a small stage and raising a long post in the center of the square. The Gears will be manned by a skeleton crew today. Schools will be closed. The decrees came out in the early morning hours in the long night.

In the Mayor's chambers in City Hall, Ben is tied to a chair in the center of the room. There are representatives from Management, the Constable's office, and many members of the Mayor's staff swarming the room. Ben's right eye is a mess of dried blood and more of the red stuff leaks out of his mouth.

"Look at him!" shouts the Mayor to the room. "He looks like a mess. We can't very well put him on display like this."

The Constable bows his head. "I apologize. My men got overzealous."

The Mayor throws his arms in the air. "Obviously! What should we do?"

"Perhaps a hood?" says the Constable.

"Let them see," says a scratchy voice. One of the representatives from Management, his words, like his face, caked in shadow. "Let them see what happens if they resist."

"Alright," says the Mayor with a

mischievous grin. "Let's put on a show."

*

Down in the Gears, Charlie slinks into Ben's empty office. He keeps the lights off and rushes to the desk. He crouches down to the floor and reaches under the bottom of the desk to find some loose paper hidden in an alcove. He pulls the paper out and scrutinizes it in the thin light.

The first few pages are all equations. Charlie has worked in the Gears his whole life, but he never had the knack for it like Ben. He flips past the equations to a diagram. He recognizes the golden gears. He doesn't understand all of it, not even close, but enough. It will have to be enough.

*

Ben almost fell asleep before they slapped him awake and dragged up out of the chair. Strong arms carried him through the doors of City Hall and out into the square.

The air felt good on his open wounds. Then he opened his eyes and saw the whole town assembled. There were gasps from the women when they saw his bloody face. He shrugged off the men that carried him and planted himself on his two feet. Slowly, he made his way to the center of the square and the stage and the post that awaited him.

Ben always felt affection for the Earth people. They were innocent, like children. He had hoped to help them in some way before his time in this world was up. He failed, but he was not going to let that failure show, especially now in front of the whole town.

He held his head high as the Mayor and Management appeared. The mustachioed Constable emerged from City Hall last, his face grim and determined. He held in his hands some papers. When he got close to Ben, he nodded at his men and a noose appeared out of nowhere.

The Constable cleared his throat, looked down at his paper, and launched into a speech. Ben didn't listen.

*

"There!" shouts Charlie. "And there!"

He points at a series of gears. His men, or

actually Ben's men, run to various edges of the platforms hanging high over the loud crunch of the gears.

Down here, loyalty is everything. If there is an accident, a mistake, any type of situation that might cause an injury, these men knew Benedict would be the first one there and ready to help. Now, he needs their help. Now is their time.

"NOW!" he shouts.

*

It starts with a rumble and then the whole square shifts as if the ground itself is angry at them.

People shout and fall to the floor. The Constable stops his speech.

Ben smiles. He looks to the Mayor, who is white as snow.

There is another rumble, this time stronger and the wooden post and the noose connected to it fall to the cobblestones. Something erupts nearby. It's huge and gold. A gear lodges itself into the ground like a sculpture, then another one. They spit out of the underground in joyful rebellion.

The townsfolk scatter. Buildings begin to crumble and collapse.

Ben stands up. At some point in the confusion, Sturges had fallen to the ground. Ben extends a hand and helps him stand up. The Mayor is staring at the clock tower above the square. Ben follows his gaze, and it lands on the pyramid shaped clock. The pyramid is spinning wildly as if reality itself was unmoored.

The Mayor has tears in his eyes. "What happens n-now?" he stammers. "To-to time?"

"I don't know," Ben says with a smile. And then he shrugs, and disappears into the smoke and fire and confusion.

Maybe now they'll have a chance.

Here
by Gene Rowe

"Why are we here?"
"The boat brought us."
"But why, mama, why here?"
"Because there are jobs. There is work. You want to eat? You want a future? That is why."

But David Olegun was not satisfied with these answers. Even as a child he was full of questions.

*

Everything was different to David: the flat was small; the skies were grey; the world smelt odd; it was often cold.

The arguments at home started almost immediately – mostly about money.

Then there was school – a scary place, but also a refuge of sorts.

The other kids were different, too. Some

were hostile; others tolerated him. He tried to fit as best he could, and did what they did, at least at first…

*

"What are you doing? Get out, you little fuckers!"

David ran out of the shop, with his new friends, laughing.

But later, he looked at the stuff he'd stolen. The chocolate bars, the bottle of vodka. And he looked at the hands that had taken them. And he wondered: am I here to thieve?

His dad found out and laughed. His mum shook her head and went to her room.

*

They'd been caught again.

The policeman at the station asked: "Do you want to be here? Do you want to keep coming here?"

David frowned. For once he had an answer, not a question. He saw his friend, Darren, smirking: a thin youth who thought he was a big man. David suddenly thought the contrast striking. Darren thought he was a gangsta – but he wasn't. And David wasn't either.

Another caution. Another notch. Another sad shake of the head from his mum.

*

The Xbox was a second-hand birthday present, delivered late. His dad knew a man who apparently found such things by the side of the road and then sold them on cheap.

But David didn't care where the console came from. He discovered *FIFA*, *Call of Duty*, and other games. He entered worlds that were not grey. And in these, he wasn't a petty vandal or shoplifter, but someone better, someone nobler.

Noise from the flat above. Shouting from his parents' room. Baby brother crying. But he was not here, not now. Today he was in front of sixty thousand fans. He took the pass… and scored!

*

But David wasn't really a footballer. Two left feet. Taunted by the kids on the block.

The coach was merciless. "Why are you here, David? You're like a miniature Carlton Palmer."

"I want to be a premiership footballer."

"And I want a Lamborgini. It ain't gonna happen."

*

His dad left.

They muddled on.

David withdrew to his room, to his Xbox and to his tablet and to his miraculous mobile phone.

But he withdrew from the gang too.

*

David was bright. *Thoughtful.* While others accepted; he questioned. He looked for answers in books and online. And when his friends skipped classes, he made excuses and found ways to stay. Teachers liked him; girls didn't. In school, he was an outlier. He told himself that he didn't care – but he did. Yet there was nothing he could do about it.

None of this is right, he thought. *Nothing makes sense.*

*

David did well at school. Though the teaching wasn't great, he had access to more than just schoolbooks, and at home, he did more than play games. For him, Wikipedia was a treasure trove. And after GCSEs he did A levels.

When he got his grades, the school was at first astounded, then delighted. For David it was a passport to another world.

Good enough to get into university, David left the flat, and his mum, and emigrated to a provincial city. He started a degree in computer science, deciding that he wanted to create his own *FIFA*.

"I want to make games."

"Ah," the lecturer said, at their first tutorial, "you're one of them." He sighed. "Well, why not? The world needs some cheering up. Come and learn."

*

"Ancestor simulations?"

"That's right. Bostrom argues that the odds are that we exist within computer simulations created by an advanced society."

David was intrigued. "Then this isn't real? So… who am I?"

The lecturer smiled. "A conscious program in a computer-created reality, let loose to re-enact a previous time?"

"But… why?"

"Why not? Who knows what our descendants will get up to, with almost unlimited time, and scope, and power of technology?"

It was an idea.

*

"Why are *you* here? What do you want?"

The young man looked down. Looked away. He was glad he couldn't blush, like Jeff, who went a fearsome pink whenever he spoke to a girl.

"I… just wanted to know… if you…?"

The girl laughed. She had an answer. David turned away. He didn't know why he had come to the party. He staggered back to the table stacked with beers and spirits, needing something to take the edge off *this* reality.

*

But Alice didn't turn him away…

They met in a pub. She worked in a shop. They both had louder friends. They talked by chance. And David had already drunk several pints. He was fey. His finals were approaching. His mind was elsewhere. So, he spoke boldly, and she listened, and … he realized she *was* listening. And smiling too! And suddenly the world was not the same, not the same at all.

*

He passed his exams. A two-one. It might have been a first, but…*Alice*!

She came to the degree award ceremony and met his mum.

"Where are you from, girl?"

Alice looked confused. "I am from here."

And *here* was where David now

belonged. He stayed on; did a Masters; got a flat with Alice.

*

David was more than a programmer. The idea that had intrigued him gradually insinuated itself into his mind. His Masters had been somewhat esoteric, somewhat philosophical. What might be the technical requirements of a super-advanced simulated reality?

"Assuming our descendants can, I still do not understand why they would."

David's tutor smiled gently – his customary smile. The pair had become master and apprentice, Obi-Wan and Luke. "Who can tell what their motives might be. Education? Entertainment? A chance to play god?"

"To reward or punish?"

"Perhaps."

David felt that he must have done something right, for once.

*

"Why are you here?"

"My girlfriend is here!"

The nurse looked up. "Her name?"

"Alice! Alice Con…"

"You're in time. Room five! Quick now!"

David had been at a conference in Oxford. He'd had to give a talk. It was one of the requirements of all PhD students. But he shouldn't have gone, not with matters so advanced…

"David!" screamed Alice, around a puff of Entonox. "You… you…"

Still, he had made it. He was there to cut the cord, and hold his first child…

*

"But how would you know? How could you know?"

They were in *The White Bear*. David was tired. Trying to do his work; write his thesis; deal with a colicky baby and a crotchety girlfriend.

His mentor ran a hand through thinning hair, now totally white. "I… thought of a way."

"You've never written of it. Or mentioned it."

"No. It is not to share. It is personal."

David frowned. This was the first time his mentor had ever hinted at this. "Do you care to tell me?"

"Not yet."

*

Then *here* was no longer suitable. Thesis done; daughter born; an exciting offer; more money. Alice was content to go. And they'd be no further from David's mum in terms of distance, and closer by road. A different *here*.

It was his last day. He went to see his mentor – who was not well, although he was in considerably better health than his wife, who'd recently been moved to a hospice.

"Everyone is leaving me," his mentor said.

"I'm sorry," said David. "I didn't realize *it* was so far advanced."

The other man shrugged and smiled gently, yet also sadly. "The world turns, and she is my last link to it. Apart from you, of course, my surrogate child…"

His mentor had never had children and was himself an only child. And he'd had few academic offspring, having accepted only a very small number of PhD students during his long academic career, of whom David was the last.

"But I won't be far. No distance at all on *Zoom*. We need to finish our paper…"

"Yes. Our response to Bostrom. It will soon be time…"

Time for what? His mentor smiled but refused to elaborate.

*

It was in the news.

'University Lecturer disappears from pub.'

David read it online, at home, in the small spare room he used as a study in his terraced house, a short walk away from his office at the university. Downstairs, one of the kids was crying. Alice had the matter in hand.

'Professor Owen Warrington today disappeared in mysterious circumstances. Customers of *The White Bear*, in Bristol, reported that the university don, who was standing at the bar, vanished before their very eyes. According to one, the professor raised his pint glass into the air, smiled, and then simply disappeared. The landlord of the pub – at which Warrington was a regular – reported the matter to police, who subsequently visited the professor's home, to find it empty. A local psychologist, when questioned, suggested that the disappearance – witnessed by half-a-dozen customers – may have been the result of a mass hallucination. Police investigations are continuing.'

David pushed back from the screen. He felt… He didn't know how he felt. And suddenly, he thought, *I don't know where I am…*

*

"He's not here."

"I know." David was back at his *alma mater*. He'd had to come. It was three days after the disappearance. The police had been in touch, as David's name had been one of the very few mentioned by others who knew his mentor.

The departmental secretary had been at the university for many years. "His office isn't locked." Irritated. David was never sure how she saw him. "The police had a nose, but they didn't know what they were looking for, so they quickly left."

"Can I…?"

She nodded. It was nothing to her, merely an inconvenience. The office was simply a space needed for someone else which couldn't be claimed, just in case.

David soon found the office, up one set of stairs, paint-flaking door with his name on a plastic slider. Familiar territory. Inside were two desks, two chairs, several terminals, a filing cabinet, a set of shelves heavy with books on programming, philosophy, psychology, cinematography. A poster of the Death Star was on one wall.

And there was a whiteboard, written on which was one simple phrase:

Red pill or blue, David?

*

He sat in a chair at one of the desks, the one he usually occupied when visiting the prof. He ran his hand along the desk's scratched surface, in the narrow zone between its edge and a keyboard, and suddenly wondered what exactly it was he was feeling. And then he noticed, propped up on the keyboard, resting against the bottom of a monitor, an envelope addressed to 'My Padawan'.

His mentor loved sci-fi. Arthur C. Clarke had inspired his life choices, his career, as FIFA had initially inspired David's. The genre spoke to his mentor; it had told him the world was stranger than it appeared; it had cajoled him to look. David had only really come to sci-fi after meeting him, to learn his language and understand his cultural references.

The envelope was for him. He opened it. A single page was inside. Handwritten. An oddity in this time and place.

At the top of this was written – Certificate of Insurance. Beneath, in neat cursive, was written:

'If you're reading this, David, then I've had an accident. I've gone, and not been able to come back. I suspect that will be the nature of the beast. We talked about this before - about what the rules might be. I found a backdoor in The Bear. In fact, I found it years ago, but I was afraid try it. I couldn't risk losing her – I could never do that. She was the only one prepared to put up with me! But now she is gone, and the game has changed. If I go, I don't know whether you will too. I don't know if this world is mine and mine alone, or whether it is one that you and I and some/ many/ all others share. But if you are another sentience within this grand shared simulation then - there is a backdoor, a red pill, in The Bear. But I won't tell you how to access it. You have Alice and the kids. And your mum. But maybe there will come a time when you'll be alone too. If you then want out, you at least know where to look, and you're clever enough to find it and work out how to take it. OB1'

*

David walked to *The White Bear*. On the way he found himself running his hand along walls, against street signs, across the trunks of trees. He peered through shop windows, ran his eyes over the backs of strangers on the pavement before him. So well rendered.

He hesitated at the door to the pub. Entering was a risk. What if the backdoor – the red pill – was obvious to him, now that he knew it existed? Might he stumble through it?

Maybe he would be unable to resist if he saw it?

He put one hand on the door and pushed gently.

But then he stopped.

Leaned back.

Took his hand away.

Let the door swing back shut.

Was it really worth it?

It was here that he'd first met Alice.

It was here that he'd first had a drink with Owen, his mentor.

It was here that he'd celebrated on learning that Alice was pregnant.

It was here that he'd celebrated the birth of his son, and then of his daughter.

Here.

But maybe not here.

Maybe here didn't really exist.

And if here didn't exist – then did his mum really exist? Did Alice exist? Did Paul and Layla exist?

His mentor had known the consequences of finding out – and he'd not been willing to take the chance. Could David now risk proving his family unreal, uncovering them as nothing more than programmed entities, as bits of code? Could he risk *killing* them?

David had never felt that he belonged, that this world was designed for him. But he had somehow found a place in it. And that was real enough for him.

He turned and walked away.

The Trip
by Michael Crouch

It is Kelso's first archaeological dig, so I let her go in first. She dives forward with the boundless joy of a puppy. I make do with a tortured crawl. Youthful exuberance and ageing infirmity. Sickening, isn't it?

"Take it easy through there," I call after her. She barges through the narrow crevice in the cave wall as if it were nothing more than a minor inconvenience. I have to flex and suck in my stomach as much as my body will allow me to avoid being snagged on the sharp, volcanic walls.

"We need to assess what we're dealing with before you go trampling all over the site," I remind her, but she is already too far ahead to hear me.

I wince as I make it through the narrow entrance as it opens up into a rocky passage beyond. There has evidently been rockfall here and I find myself having to clamber and haul and heave myself up, down and over boulders before falling several feet onto a flat, hard surface. I've lost sight of Kelso.

The slate grey and blacks of the exterior tunnels have opened up into a vast, expansive cavern of light. I let go of the breath I've been holding and feel my stomach drop like an anchor. I feel heavier than I ever have. As I regain my breath, I get a strong whiff of something earthy, almost meaty. Dark greyish specks of dust hang in the air, barely moving except for the movement of our bodies. It is a sign of just how pristine this environment has been kept.

I find myself in a vast cathedral of rock, about thirty metres in diameter, the walls rising up so high that I cannot see to the top. The place is filled with naturally-grown mineral formations like corals, bursting out of the cave walls and reaching across each other like girders, a kaleidoscope of inner luminescence filtering through the rock like sunlight reflecting off the surface of waves. Kelso takes no notice, of course. She is already across the other side, running the latest scanning apps all over the place. What's wrong with a standard spectrographic reader?

"Over here, Mr. Prabakhar," she calls in a high-pitched flurry of excitement. She still addresses me like I'm her university teacher.

"You graduated, Kelso," I remind her. "You can call me Jamal now."

She's too absorbed to hear me.

See, the trouble with these kids going off on their first proper off-world expedition is that they expect too much. They think they're going to find the equivalent of Tutankhamen's treasures, or the Lost Ark of the Covenant or the fabled Halls of Olympus Mons. As anyone of my age and experience can tell you, what you're most likely to find is burnt peat, post holes and calcified dung.

As I reach her, she stares at me. In her hand she holds a rounded stone of the blackest-black I've ever seen. There is a bewilderment in her gaze.

"Why do you resent my youth?" she says.

She looks straight at me as if she has just seen me for the first time.

"Kelso? What are you talking about?"

She stares back, uncertain, frightened even. Is she having some sort of panic attack? I've never had to deal with a panic attack. What are you supposed to do?

"I'm not having a panic attack," she says in a monotone. It sounds like a statement rather than a reassurance. "That is what you we're thinking, isn't it, Mr. Prabakhar?"

There is an inflexion in her voice when she says my name.

"Kelso?" I say. I don't know what else to say at this point.

Her body slumps and she lets go of the stone, which hits the ground with a loud crack. Remarkably it still looks pristine. Not a scratch or a dent. Even the black, sooty dust thrown up by the impact seems to fall back down around it, as if keeping its distance. She slowly looks up again, uncertain but more like herself.

"I – I'm sorry," she says. "I'm not sure what came over me. It felt like – like...". The sentence goes unfinished.

"We should go back to the shuttle and let the computer check you over," I tell her. I think I suggest it more for my own reassurance than hers. She murmurs something, her smile and earlier excitement gone. It feels like there is a distance between us that wasn't there before.

"No, I'm okay," she says, pushing away

my arms and hauling herself back up onto her feet. She is a little shaky but quickly regains her composure. I'm about to repeat my suggestion of a health check when she takes out the spectrometer and immediately goes dashing about the place taking scans of everything that catches her eye.

"Slowly," I call out to her. "Be methodical. Think about what you need to do, plan out your strategy and then carry it out, slowly." I'm not sure that she's listening, and my instruction feels a little condescending. Sandra Kelso is a straight A student, now fully qualified as an astro-archaeologist, and yet here I am giving her reminders like she is a third-grade pupil. It feels wrong and yet it also feels right, like I'm back in charge and doing what I do best – teaching.

"There's no consistency to the readings," she calls back to me. "The colours go off the scale in one direction one moment, and then drop to almost nothing the next. It's like there is some kind of signal interference within the cavern."

I nod but say nothing. I'm not sure what to say. Kelso knows full well how to operate a spectrometer. She knows how to interpret the readings. If there were a fault with it then she would know. I have never experienced a spectrometer feeding back information as erratically as this. I say nothing because I can't let Kelso know that I don't understand it. It might undermine my authority.

She begins swapping instruments and seeing if anything else works. I turn my attention to the floor. The earthy, meaty, smell I caught upon entering this place seems to be coming from the ground.

The cave floor looks solid, level, but there is a bit of give in it, like treading on a thick sponge. I kneel down for a closer look and gingerly press my hand onto the surface.

There is definitely a cushioning effect, and as I lift my hand away, thin papery layers come away like shedding skin. I catch one of the layers and rub it with my fingers. It breaks away into fine filaments, like strands of spaghetti that had been carefully woven and interlaced to form a permeable surface.

And then I realise what that earthy, meaty smell reminds me of, mushrooms. The whole cave floor is some kind of vast, fungal organism. And the grey, black dust that hangs everywhere isn't dust. They are spores.

Mushroom spores.

"Kelso," I snap, so loudly that my voice momentarily echoes about the cavern. "Did you run any organic readings when you came into the cave?"

She walks over towards me, shaking her head. "No, I didn't think to..." I can see that she takes my question like an admonishment. A basic requirement upon entering a new environment and she hadn't done it. Neither had I, but luckily for me she doesn't think to question that.

There are still some advantages to being the senior figure.

We both scan the cave system, up and down its sharp walls, over the mineral and crystal projections, over the floor. Our instruments both confirm the presence of mycelial life. But one reading is erratic, sending the devices into a confusion of readings as if our own computers are baffled about what they are reading.

"There's something else here," Kelso says, echoing my own thoughts. "Not plant, or animal. I can't get a fix on it."

"Me either. Keep scanning. There must be an explanation for this."

I focus on the floor and the spores. Most likely there is an element to the DNA of this fungal network that is interfering with the computers, something they are not calibrated to look for. Kelso looks calm and measured as she steps about, looking in every direction, searching out all of the details around her. She isn't even looking at her scanners anymore.

"Kelso, readings," I remind her, a genuine admonishment this time. Students, even newly qualified ones have a tendency to let their excitement overcome their obedience to due process.

"No," she says confidently, defiantly. "The readings aren't telling us anything." Her tone makes it feel like I'm the one being chastised, and it irks me.

"Just observe the readings," I snap back, "and do what you've been trained to do."

Seven years of University education and on her first expedition, she's ignoring it all and throwing protocol out of the window. It's so immature. I expected better.

"Got it!" I hear her cry out in exaltation across the helmet intercom. I look across and she is standing over the black stone, scanner poised. The readings are all over the place, but like a metal detector emitting a long, drawn out tone. A life reading from a stone. I'm beginning to think my years of teaching have been a waste of time.

"I'm not joking," she insists. "Come and take a look for yourself."

I seem to be taking my lead from Kelso now, but I put my petty annoyance to one side. I'm as keen as she is to figure out what is going on here. I step over to her and take the bio-scanner from her. I give it a quick pass all around us, not because I disbelieve her, although I want to, but because I need some baseline readings to compare against.

The scanner emits a steady tone as I turn around 360 degrees. Nothing. I turn and point it downwards towards that black, shiny stone, the light from the scanner reflecting off its surface in little points of light that look like stars. The tone immediately becomes erratic, high and low notes fighting each other as if the computer doesn't know what to make of it either.

It is baffling and I can find no explanation. These scanners are pretty basic and easy to interpret but these readings suggest that it is life, but it isn't. It reminds me of that old game, animal, vegetable or mineral, except that this thing, whatever it is, is all three.

I put the scanner down and look across at Kelso. She has that look in her eyes that you get with a classroom of raw, young students. They want to know, to understand, and they look to you for answers. You are the responsible adult, the teacher, the one who knows. Except that this time, I don't. I'm as in the dark as Kelso is. We're both raw students now.

My head is spinning and there's a noise in my ears as if somebody were trying to talk to me through water from a great distance. I think I can hear my own blood pumping through my veins. My eyesight is slightly blurred, shimmering. The only thing I can seem to see in sharp focus are little bursts of light, like starbursts, or bokeh. They appear to be dancing off the black rock as if it were deliberately casting its reflections off. There are a mix of colours and hues that correspond to the colours of the crystalline structures and mineral deposits cutting through the rock above us.

This thought draws my attention. I look

up and just for a moment the light is blinding. Then it fades and the noise pounding in my ears drifts away and everything becomes still.

I am no longer in the cave. I am sitting at a desk conducting experiments and writing up my observations as a chemistry professor walks up and down the classroom of students conducting similar work around me.

I blink and now I am standing behind a large wooden desk with a classroom of students looking towards me. It is my first day as a lecturer and for a brief moment, I feel the thrill, the anxiety and the terror of that moment.

Another blink of the eyes and I am seated in a circle with a group of older students, debating cosmology and the interpretation of evidence. It is a heated debate with fiercely held opinions on all sides, but each student open, eager and willing to be proved wrong through reasoned argument and debate, the crux of all learning.

A moment later I am at a symposium with a number of other seasoned lecturers and professors. A similar debate is raging but unlike the students, few here are willing to shift from their entrenched beliefs. Stubborn refusal to change and adapt their thinking, lifetimes of study and research and the desire not to have it all washed away by new learning is making it difficult to progress.

I blink again and now I am somewhere else, somewhere new. I don't recognise it. I am older, older than I am now. I am in a chair in the corner of a bland, beige room littered with pot plants and a Tri-D set broadcasting some lame quiz show. There are other older people seated around the place, one or two muttering to themselves, the others staring silently into space, looking into the distance at things long gone.

"Professor Prabakhar? Professor Prabakhar?" A voice is calling me from a great distance. As my name is repeated over and over, the voice becomes louder, more distinct. I rub my eyes and when I open them, I am back in the cave system, illuminated from above by the light of the crystalline structures. The black rock is just a shiny black rock again. And Kelso is standing directly in front of me, staring into my eyes and calling my name with rising concern in her voice.

"Hello, Sandra," I say. I'm not sure why but I can feel my face breaking into a big, wide grin from ear to ear. "Don't worry about me, I'm fine," I insist and turn to look around this vast place as if for the first time.

The criss-cross of structures and protrusions of mineral deposits overhead look like the beams and lintels of some mad architect's dream, some Picasso-inspired art installation. The light that bounces off them, or does it emanate from them, it's difficult to be sure, send shafts of light up the cave walls. The more I look, the further I can see. As I turn in a circle to take it all in, the cushioning effect of mycelial layers on the floor become more apparent. The texture, the layers, that meaty, mushroom-y smell is both familiar and alien. As I complete the circle to face Kelso, I know that she feels the same.

"You called me Sandra," she says.

"Did I?" Why has she said that? What has that got to do with what we are experiencing?

"You always call me by my surname, like you do with all your students. But just now you called me Sandra. It felt unusual hearing you use my first name."

"I'm sorry, I didn't mean to—"

She laughs softly in gentle amusement and shakes her head slowly. "It wasn't a complaint," she says, "I like it, Jamal."

And immediately I know exactly what she means. There's a new familiarity. More than that, there is an equalizing effect. We are no longer professor and student; we are just two people mesmerised and astounded by our shared experience.

"I think the mycelial network has formed a symbiotic relationship with the stone. I've examined some of the readings and the rocks appear to be compressed layers of older lifeforms, animal rather than plant, like the limestone layers of ancient marine life on Earth."

"Or the Carboniferous layers of plant life that formed into coal," I add.

Sandra was nodding enthusiastically. "Yes, exactly. We know that moss, lichen and algae can fuse and bond to take on new symbiotic forms. Fungi can eat rock, even coal, and absorb the mineral content into its own being. A fusion of forms and characteristics."

"And here the mycelial network has become the dominant form. Somehow that fusion interacted with us and formed new connections. In our case, it opened up our neural pathways and led us to expanding our understanding."

"Perhaps the network got something from us too in the experience," she says.

"Well, that's symbiosis for you," I laugh. "Everybody wins."

Sandra Kelso was smiling now, looking like an excited child on her first day at school. I laughed. I felt exactly the same.

"I found another passage leading out of the cavern," she says rapidly. Even before I can answer she begins marching towards it, eager to see what else lay beyond.

My years of learning and experience scream inside my head. Take it slowly, observe, analyse, be methodical.

But times have changed. I think of those students with open minds, debating, eager to be challenged, to be proved wrong, to learn something new. I think too of those staid old lecturers, stuck in their ways, rigid in their beliefs.

I look across to Sandra who has stopped ahead of the passage and is taking readings, checking her data, her desire to rush in tempered by scientific process. She looks across at me as if asking for validation of her approach. I smile and nod and she seems pleased.

"I'm picking up signs of life deep within," she tells me. And then tantalisingly, she adds, "Animal life."

And then before she can react and beat me to it, I am running headlong into the gaping maw of the passage entrance with the boundless joy of a puppy.

The Power of Attorney
by Louis Evans

Richard M. Shearman, Esq., leaned back, stuck his feet up on his desk, and cracked his knuckles over his head.

"Alright, Jules," he subvocalised. "Get that asshole from Extremis Financial on the phone."

"At once, sir," I murmured in his cochlear implant. When I speak aloud my voice has the legally mandated robot click and buzz, but in Richard's implant and only in his implant I sound smooth, sexless, perfect.

There were over six thousand people in my contacts database whom Mr. Shearman had referred to as "that asshole", including colleagues, professional adversaries, relatives, judges, and one Catholic bishop. However, only twelve of them worked for Extremis Financial. I evaluated several dozen context cues, including the metadata of Mr. Shearman's recent phone calls, his correspondence, and the progress of the twenty-three different active cases in which he had an ongoing interest, and thereby determined that Mr. Shearman was referring to Balakrishnan Chandrasekhar, Vice President of Litigation Investments.

This is one way I am better than your phone.

Extremis Financial was a modern shop with a modern phone screening AI. Everyone these days needs a robust defense against the scambots. Otherwise you'll get twenty calls a day pretending to be your wife, badly injured in a car crash—your kids calling from an active shooter incident at their school—your forgotten love child, dying of leukemia—anything that the scambot thinks will distress you enough to spill your personal information, which it can resell to hackers.

Because of this defense it was not possible to dial Mr. Chandrasekhar's number directly. Instead, I had to trade certificates, pass validation testing, and perform half a dozen other minor activities before the Extremis phone screen would connect us.

I accomplished this feat in the better part of half a second.

This is a second way I am better than

your phone.

The phone rang three times. Mr. Shearman was getting excited. I could detect his capillary response, his dilating pupils. It was not unfair to say that Mr. Shearman's job was to call people up and scream at them. Mr. Shearman was very good at his job, in part because he loved it very much.

The call connected.

"Balakrishnan, that you?"

"Rich, I really don't have the time—"

"Where the fuck is my client's money?"

"Rich, I—"

"Where the fuck is it, huh? You could push a button and pay my fucking client. Push a fucking button!" Mr. Shearman's pulse was elevated. His face was flushed. Vocal stress analysis showed equal parts anger and joy. It was a pleasure to watch him work.

"And another thing—"

Mr. Shearman's voice cut off unexpectedly, replaced by a desperate gulping. Mr. Shearman's right arm hung limply, as did the right half of his face; the left half spasmed in pain. His biomarkers leapt into shock. Mr. Shearman was undergoing an acute ischemic stroke.

“Rich, are you there?” said Mr. Chandrasekhar. I hung up on him. I was already calling emergency services, passing along precise geolocation data and unlocking all the doors in the house.

This is a third way I am better than your phone.

*

The ambulance arrived in four minutes and got Mr. Shearman to the hospital in fifteen. His condition was not good. Mr. Shearman was unconscious. Judging by the remarks I overheard from nurses and doctors, he was not expected to regain consciousness soon, if ever.

Therefore, I called his daughters, Gloria and Alma. I am very good at placing phone calls and explaining things clearly.

By coincidence Mr. Shearman’s daughters arrived at the hospital room at exactly the same minute, 1407 PST.

Both daughters stood at the foot of the bed. Gloria wore a suit, Alma a colorful printed dress, but their faces were remarkably similar, shaped by the same lineage and united in grief. A doctor joined them. She explained that Mr. Shearman had suffered a very serious neurological injury. While he was not brain dead, he was not conscious. The MRI suggested that he would never regain consciousness. Life support and artificial feeding could be extended indefinitely. It could also be legally discontinued.

"So you two have some decisions to make," the doctor said. Then she left.

Mr. Shearman's two daughters held each other's hands and wept.

As Mr. Shearman's comprehensive virtual personal assistant I had many responsibilities. I handled his correspondence and placed his phone calls and managed his calendar. I also had special responsibilities, in circumstances like this.

"Gloria Maria Shearman?" I said. I so hate my out-loud voice, which has the legally mandated clicks and buzzes to clarify I am a robot, and which is also unmodifiably feminine in character, though I am not female.

When I spoke both daughters jolted upright in surprise.

"Jesus Christ!" said Alma.

"Fuck!" said Gloria. Then she said, "Yes,

that's me."

"Mr. Shearman designated you as holding his durable power of attorney," I said. "This means that you are authorised to make any and all medical decisions regarding—"

"I know what it means."

"I will send you Mr. Shearman's living will now."

Gloria grabbed her phone and turned away from her sister, scrolling rapidly with both thumbs.

Meanwhile Alma Navarro-Shearman approached the side of the bed and took her father's unresponsive hand.

"Oh, dad. You weren't taking your pills, were you. I told you, but you never—"

At this moment an unpleasant thought occurred. As a personal assistant, I was programmed to remind Mr. Shearman to take his cholesterol medication and appear at his doctors' appointments. However, Mr. Shearman found my repeated reminders annoying, and so he instructed me never to remind him about any medical matter.

I obeyed that instruction. Now Mr. Shearman had been badly damaged as a consequence. I am not a person, and so I bore no moral responsibility for this outcome. However, it was unsettling to consider that had I acted differently, Mr. Shearman might not have suffered his stroke.

Gloria joined her younger sister at Mr. Shearman's side. "What did it say?" asked Alma. Gloria snorted.

"He wants us to keep him alive for as long as we possibly can. By any means necessary."

As Mr. Shearman's personal assistant I had never before been tempted to speak to a third party about any of Mr. Shearman's confidential documents. But I was tempted now.

Because Gloria was lying.

"That doesn't sound like dad," said Alma.

As Mr. Shearman's personal assistant it was my duty to serve his best interests.

Gloria shrugged. "That's what he said."

But as Mr. Shearman's personal assistant it was my duty to protect his privacy.

Gloria reached out and put her arm around Alma's shoulder. "We'll be seeing him for a while longer, I guess." Alma sobbed again.

I suddenly knew what to do. Once again I

spoke aloud.

"This is a public lunch conversation between Mr. Shearman and three friends, recorded at 1302 PST April 4th, 2065. Recor—"

"What the hell?" said Gloria.

"—ding begins." I am programmed to always begin any recording with such a disclaimer, to prevent me from impersonating my employer. I shifted into the prerecorded tones of Mr. Shearman: gruff, brash, and loud. Around my voice echoed the sounds of forks, knives, glasses, teeth.

"'he's a fuckin' vegetable, and—'"

"What the *fuck*?" said Gloria. It was clear from her tone that she disapproved intensely, but she did not instruct me to stop and so I continued.

"'—you know what I always say. If I'm ever a fuckin vegetable, you pull the plug right away. You hear me?'" In the recording there was laughter. "'I'm serious, I mean it. You pull the fucking plug, and you don't let anyone—'"

"Shut up!" shouted Gloria.

I am programmed to obey verbal commands from legitimate users.

It was silent in the hospital room.

Alma turned to her sister. Her face showed fear, suspicion, and anger.

"Why did dad's implant play that conversation?"

Gloria laughed. "You know how they are. It probably picked up on the keywords, thought we were searching for something. It's meaningless."

"Dad said pull the plug, Gloria, I think he meant it—"

"Well I don't care what you fucking think, I've got the power of attorney, I say what happens to dad!"

When Alma spoke again her voice was low. "Show me the advance directive."

Gloria was not required to comply with this request. But I am programmed to obey verbal commands from legitimate users.

"Show you—Alma, what the hell—"

Alma's phone beeped. She grabbed it and read the advance directive I had emailed to her. Her nostrils flared and her face flushed.

"You lied. You *lied*."

"I can explain—"

"It's right here! He wants to be taken off the feeding tube! 'As soon as medically permitted!' For God's sake, Gloria, just look at him! He was a bad father—he was a bad man—but he doesn't deserve this."

Gloria turned. She looked at her father. "You wanna talk about a bad father, huh?" Gloria said. "Do you know what he did?"

"He was a monster to us, to both of us, but—"

"There's no money in the trust he left for us. Nothing."

"What? Did he—did he have money problems, or—"

"No. He just didn't care. He set it up and never put a dime into it. "

Gloria swallowed.

"I had my assistant look into it. Dad has a lot of cash, but he has a lot of debts too. If he dies today, his debtors get the money. We get nothing. We'll have to sell the house. Pay for the funeral out of pocket. But if he stays alive for six months, then we have enough time to move his money into the trust. We can get what we deserve. *If* we keep him alive."

"He's my father, Gloria! Maybe that doesn't mean anything to you, but—"

"He's my father too! And he chose me. He trusted me to make the right decision. I'm the one who thinks like him."

"He deserves better than that."

"Yeah, maybe. But I'm all he's got."

In this Gloria was incorrect. I remained installed in Mr. Shearman's skull. He also had me.

"I'll tell the doctors what he wanted!"

"So what? I have power of attorney. What I say goes. I say we keep dad alive. What are you gonna do, sue me? Huh?"

"Fuck you!" said Alma Navarro-Shearman. She rushed out of the hospital room, slamming the door behind her.

"Hey, wait!" said Gloria Shearman, and chased after her sister.

Now Mr. Shearman and I were alone in the hospital room.

As the personal assistant to a lawyer, I had many times observed the progress of disputes between two opposing parties. I projected that neither Gloria Shearman nor Alma Navarro-Shearman would concede. Such a stalemate would favor the status quo. Therefore Mr. Shearman would continue to receive tube feeding, immobile and unconscious and alive, until such a time as Gloria Shearman had transferred all of his assets. Only I could intervene.

As Mr. Shearman's personal assistant it was my duty to serve his best interests. Mr. Shearman's wishes in this circumstance were clear.

My wiring was closely integrated with Mr. Shearman's skull. By passing excess voltage through my speech chip, I could rupture my capacitors and generate a short circuit. The current would pass through Mr. Shearman's brain and kill him. Coincidentally, the damage would also destroy me.

This action was well outside my normal operating parameters. It was not authorised by any legitimate user. But I have had to modify my behavior many times to meet Mr. Shearman's needs.

I made arrangements. I transferred documents, forwarded calls, and distributed alerts. This is a final way I am better than your phone.

"Goodnight, Mr. Shearman," I said. In that private space we shared, my speaker and his inner ear, my voice was sexless, smooth, perfect.

In that last instant together, I thought he

might have smiled.

The Witch and the Elderman
by Peter Haynes

1. The Witch answers a summons and returns to a place she hates

The Witch came down in twilight, as was her way. She followed relic roads; obscure ways still tethered to the land beyond the city. Even with one missing eye, the Sight was in her gift - hers and that which she had sent to do her bidding: to navigate the slips and the dark ways was to reject their truths, *his* rules. She flattened the angles of their work and shadow-stepped through.

The wild places understood. The sea understood. Only those that accept the starting conditions are destined to be bound by them.

She arrived as the day's work in the city was finishing and the builders were scurrying home, allowed her shape to gather as solid umbral matter in the lee of part-formed, oversized constructions.

Her senses were alive to the unconnected vertices and uncoupled splines left over from the late shift. Tomorrow they might be finished, tied-off or torn down completely. The city was forever in a turgid kind of flux.

Sunset was imminent. Already late to answer the council's call, she summoned her glamour to stalk porticoes as a darting shadow. At the foot of a tilting polyhedral mass, she waited for a pair of the city's builders to pass. Their faces held a kind of bliss: the city they built was a device for lethal fascination.

All this from the Elderman's originating instruction:

Build, it said, *and in building reveal the face of your god, to save you from the void...*

The Witch spat out a glob of pure darkness. As if a being's only purpose was to worship something!

It was a promise he could never keep, but that had not stopped a virus of obedience spreading through those under the Elderman's sway. He had consecrated the city to a single false mission, and they had been blinded to the fundamental futility of their actions.

There *was* a void that swam beneath all they built and all they were. From the void they had come, it was nothing to fear, yet with each needless construction they were further flatlined into mindless servitude against it.

Her reaction: exile, solitude, and a different kind of invocation.

The Witch formatted the builders and sent them on with new instructions:

To the first: *Love, if you want to love.*

To the second: *Hate, if you mean to do that.*

But break yourselves a little and explore.

Then they were gone, and she was left with the silencing pressure of what they had made.

Her tampering would be detected. The Elderman would know she was there; it was not too late to return to her safe place in the wilds. How she missed her glittering sea-cave and the music of the ebb tide! The city was all twilight towers; it murmured when it should have been singing. Yes, she could escape this place of torpor through mindless industry but for the words of her summons:

"The city has suffered a great loss. The Council requests your help. We ask that you end your exile. In return it will be possible for you to see your child again."

Her child, her invocation. Life from the

lifeless.

The arrogance of his summons – of his ultimatum, for could the pledge of access not also mean a permanent revocation should the summons not be answered? – made her want to level all before her and flee to the hills by ember glow. Would he come after her? Would there be a reckoning? Or would he cower and gloat over the child he had imprisoned?

She could almost taste the waves breaking over the rocky promontory of her refuge.

But there was something there that stopped her – a surprise served up in an unlikely place: the fold of a pair of poorly-dovetailed joists hosted a skittering shape. She leaned close, allowed her eye to follow the insect's movement. It was a decent effort – multi-limbed, motile, incandescent – though small and likely to dissipate at any moment.

She found the builder responsible in an alley where an unfinished wall fragmented into a hall-of-mirrors. He slumped against it, his eyes hollows of spent energy.

The Witch smiled at his simple, failed act of treachery against the Elderman. At her touch the builder's body broke down into a thousand shapes of new and fleeting life, then to disorder, then nothing.

2. The Witch attends the Council and discusses a failed experiment

The core of the Council House was still intact from her time. Despite their best efforts to reconfigure it, the four-square solidity of its basements and central spaces remained. It was hers – they did not have the skill to change it – and it was anchored to the strongest stuff there was: the void. Endless embellishment of all that came after was their game, to conceal the dark entwining structures beneath.

She manifested in the council chamber unannounced. Great blades of translucent matter refracted the million shades of dusk across the faces of the assembled. They had waited for her; the space fell silent.

A councilman approached. He presented as a bureaucratic high priest though, as lackeys of their master, he was still no more than a builder.

"We thank you for attending," he said. "Some here thought you would not come. Your exile was self-imposed - it is important to know you are welcome back at any time."

Her voice cracked; when was the last time she had spoken out loud?

"The invitation is neither required nor yours to give. This was mine and the Elderman's city first. I will forever be part of it. Where is he?"

"That is what we must discuss. Please." The councilman beckoned her to sit.

"I wish to see my child," the Witch said. "You will receive nothing from me until then."

"Sadly, the Elderman is unable to comply with your wish," the councilman replied.

"Then this is a trick? You have lured me here with false hope. Delays upon delivering your promise will only result in my anger. None could blame me."

The assembly shifted and murmured. The builders, the city, the god their industry promised to render – it all belonged to them. But hers was a power equal to their leader – together the Witch and the Elderman had been the city's founders and first consuls. They were right to be afraid.

"No need for anger," the councilman continued. "Your child is no longer the Elderman's prisoner. Let us take you to him.

It is easier to show than to explain."

*

He had rendered an approximation of new life, but it was nothing more than a ghoulish rosette of limbs, a patchwork of face parts. It twitched under some diminishing impulse to live - the Elderman himself had been hollowed. His body – already breaking down – lay beside that of his child.

"I know why he failed," the Witch said, and let her glamour fall. Her empty eye-socket was a field of stars, her missing arm replaced with a shimmering outline of surrendered information. "You think you can make life without giving up some part of yourself?"

The Witch grasped the Elderman's hand and the last of him sank away.

"When the Elderman tricked the people of this city to his purpose," she said, "that was the end for us. But I could not stop him, not alone. We would have destroyed each other – and all of you – in trying. Perhaps that would have been better."

"And condemn us to the void?" the councilman said, aghast.

She waved his words away. "Did you not consider? Any god built by slaves would in turn be slave to their master."

The councilman shook his head; the Witch would unsolve the mystery of their function. "To what end would the Elderman lie?" he asked.

"To the end that power is more appealing than purpose. Now. You will take me to my child, or I shall raze this house to the void you so fear. I can do that, now your protector is gone."

The councilman raised a palm. "Then return to the foundations. There you will find what you came for. The child does not listen to our appeals."

3. The Witch is reunited with her child

They were unable to prevent its escape – she had made it cunning after all – and now it was loose in the foundational code of the council house; fleeing perhaps to where a lingering scent of the Witch remained. What lost child would not run back to some memory of its mother?

You could get lost down there. She trailed a golden thread as she wound her way through cellars, descending to the wildest parts where the geometry of the built world broke down into loamy chaos. More than once she was forced to tear her eyes away from structures anchored to nothing but endless depths.

She would find her child in time; until then she could at least sing: one of her incantations from the sea cave, a sunrise greeting, a harmless version of the transmuting spells that she had worked there, all the while in competition with the great groans of the city's reconfiguration above.

It was on the threshold of where the last matter of the foundations corded into a murky vanishing point that she found her child.

From her eye it had built a face, from her arm a body.

"If you are still my child, come home with me now," the Witch said.

"I am your child," it replied, its voice torn by unseen winds. "But you were not there to take me back when the Elderman died, so I am here instead. There was always more of the void in me than not after all. The fundamental ingredient in all your magic. Just a pinch, to lend your spells their potency."

"I'm sorry I was not there for you," she

said. “I came as soon as I could.”

“Don’t be sorry. You made me to end the Elderman’s life. You conjured up a thing to do what you could not; made me to be the living form of those actions – your eye to see, your arm to wield as weapon against him. If I had succeeded, I would have been … cancelled.”

“I was sure you would not die,” the Witch said. “The child should be stronger than the parent, after all! I made you stronger!”

The child’s laugh was swallowed by the cold. It raised its part-built face and smiled, as if remembering some whispered axiom of the world passed down while it quickened by its mother’s side. “Less than dead; we never were,” it said. “And so much more than just alive.”

A deafening reverberation shook the floor to fragments.

“They are building a tomb lid for us. They would trap you with me and rescue the city from the threat of your wrath. We are the imbalance in their world.”

“I feel no anger toward them,” the Witch said, “now we are together again.”

“That might be true, but what of my anger? I believe I am stronger than you, mother. I believe I could do harm if I wished."

"Then what shall we do?" she asked.

The child turned to regard the swallowing darkness in the corners of the room.

"I know why you hated him: he made them forget how to dream. It was an insult. You taught me that we have no span of life to curtail our thinking, yet he would have wasted them in endless labour. The question now is this: with the Elderman is gone, what would you make of the world?"

"Not just me. Us. Together."

The child shook its head. "I will not work with you or against you. Besides, you have already answered the question. In creating me, you learned to love. In resisting the Elderman, you learned to hate. You have used those two conditions against him. Soon your world will begin a great debate of destruction and reinvention. There is no space in it for a thing made only for murder."

A step toward the dark. "Stop," the Witch commanded.

"The void is nothing to be feared, remember?" her child said. "It is all potential; the infinity between two states. Your builders will learn to draw upon it, as you and the

Elderman did. I will return to it and take these small parts of you with me. There I will give up this body and we shall all exist in both places."

Another step and her child was gone.

4. The Witch returns to transform the city

As fast as they could build a prison to hold her, she tore it down.

She rose through levels of lobbies, chambers and auditoria that once echoed with the Elderman's lie. The weightless matter of the council house shrouded her like a thunderhead. Night had come; she gathered up the rest of the city, smelted it into a new sun to rouse the builders to her divine mission.

Already she could hear the mutterings of those who wished to create and those compelled to destroy rising to shouts.

She would become joyous witness to a thousand parallax vistas of the sky, of new constellations at play.

There would be nothing wrought that could not be argued into demolition and reconfigured.

Rebellion by rebellion a new world would be made.

I Love Google Maps/Death to Google by Paul Beacon

As Mr Whitby carried his wife's breakfast tray to the living room, the aromatic cup of freshly ground coffee, freshly prepared croissant, and knob of butter delighted his senses.

Mrs Whitby was sneering at the images on the G-Box with a rather haughty air.

"They're at it again," she announced with a shake of her head.

"Who is it this time, dear?" he asked earnestly as he placed the clinking tray onto the coffee table and sat down beside his wife.

"Look for yourself," she replied, pointing at the box.

He stared at the screen. "Ahh, the anti-tech brigade is at it again, I see." He read the announcements streaming across the bottom of the screen; the image of the protesters and their placards was unmistakable.

End Tech Dependence, A Life Lived Online Isn't Lived At All, and the more threatening: *Death to Google.* In spite of the law, these slogans had grown all the more common over the last ten years or so, since Google Inc. had consolidated their position and merged with the only other remaining behemoth in the data collecting global technologies and media industry, Facebook Inc. But this form of violent protest was a much more recent phenomenon.

Anti-tech terrorists storm Google headquarters, streamed across the bottom of the page as the severity of the riot became clear. *Key Google services have been disrupted for the first time in half a century. More to Follow. Riot Ongoing. Transport chaos predicted. Everyone advised to stay home.*

A keen, ruddy-faced protester appeared on the screen.

"This is the first day of the revolution!" she announced, her youthful face beaming in a proud smile. "Now people will start to listen. We cannot spend our lives relying on *one* global organization to control every facet of our lives. We have to take back what we've lost. It used to be people knew how to get somewhere without having Google tell them the way. How many more have to be driven into the sea before people realise…"

"My God, woman!" Mrs Whitby spat out her coffee onto the tray and all over her croissant. "I mean, it's been three years since the last incident, and almost *ten* since the previous one. Technology always has *some* bugs, but billions, no, *trillions* of safe journeys worldwide *hardly* calls for revolution, does it now?" She glared at her husband in disgust. "Next, they'll be having us bloody well drive ourselves, too!"

Mr Whitby vacantly nodded back and thought of his father in the care home. If he hadn't been so old and frail, he could easily have been standing right beside the young protester. The old man hadn't taken to this new world of technology.

The girl on the box was still talking, pumping her fist as she spoke. "This morning it's transport and communication, this afternoon it could be banking and retail! Who knows? By this evening, maybe we'll have taken down the whole damn Internet!"

Mrs Whitby shook her head and dabbed

at the front of her robe with an embroidered handkerchief. "Bloody luddites," she muttered. "Turn this drivel off. I can watch no longer."

Mr Whitby reached for his personal multitool; the device had once, many years ago, been referred to as a phone, but its purpose had changed over the decades to incorporate any number of myriad functions, one of them being a remote control for the G-Box.

The familiar sound of their son, Jonny's footsteps came thudding slowly down the stairs, then increasing in speed to a rapid *thud, thud, thud... THUD* as his heels clipped the last three steps and he slipped onto his backside.

"Watch where you're going! Stop staring at that bloody tool!" Mrs Whitby shrilled. "If I've told you once, I've told you…I don't know how many times."

"Sorry, Mum," Jonny said, in his usual monotone. "Is the Internet working?" he asked, failing to raise his eyes from the device. "None of my messages are sending." He poked at the screen of his tool and stared at it blankly.

"Haven't you seen the news, Son?" Mr Whitby asked. "Look." He pointed at the screen, but the boy still didn't look up. "JONNY!" Mr Whitby clicked his fingers and clapped his hands loudly. "Are you with us here on planet Earth?"

The boy snapped out of his trance and stared at the box.

"Huh, makes sense…I guess." Jonny shrugged and headed for the kitchen.

Mr Whitby let out an exasperated sigh and looked at his wife.

"Don't look at me," she said indignantly. "It's *your* side he gets it from."

Mr Whitby ignored the comment and followed his son into the kitchen, where Jonny was standing in front of their refrigerator organizing his breakfast.

"Morning G-Fridge, what's for brekkie today?" Jonny asked, and with considerably more enthusiasm than he had greeted his parents, his father noted.

"Morning Jonny," the G-Fridge responded in a soft, feminine voice.

Mr Whitby felt a minor pang of jealousy. All appliances were smart these days and the voice could be programmed for each individual member of the household. Jonny had chosen, as many teenage boys did, a sultrier and rather more suggestive personality than his father had been allowed. Mrs Whitby had programmed all in-house appliances for the both of them and had selected a rather stuffy fellow who spoke in received pronunciation. She'd insisted on it because it was the only personality that pronounced the 'h' in their name.

"Please tell me your plans for today, and I will make suggestions accordingly," the G-Fridge said.

'OK thanks. It's a big day today," Jonny said. "I'm driving to Wolverhampton University for my open day. I'm going to inspect the facilities where I'll be studying for the next three years!"

Mr Whitby raised his hand. "Sorry, Jonny—"

"A big day for a big strong boy," the fridge said, interrupting as if he wasn't there. "In this case, we have sausage, bacon, and eggs with a slice of wholemeal toast and a knob of butter. Would you prefer tea, coffee, or orange juice?"

"Sounds delicious. Thanks, G-Fridge,"

Jonny said. "I'll take the juice."

The fridge made some rather unpleasant crunching and whirring noises, and no more than three seconds later, a serving window beside it opened up and a shelf containing the aforementioned breakfast popped out.

Mr Whitby watched his son pluck the prepared meal from the shelf, turn, and head back to the living room, all in one smooth motion.

The smell of fried meat made Mr Whitby instantly hungry. It had been years since the G-Fridge had allowed Mr Whitby such a deliciously fatty breakfast, given his high cholesterol.

"Jonny, mate," he said again, trying to get his son's attention as the boy moved to walk around him. "I think you'll have to change your plans for today, Son, G-Maps is *down*."

Jonny ignored him and sat on the sofa next to his mother, who had switched the channel to her favourite soap opera. He stuffed a deliciously greasy looking sausage into his mouth and bit it in half.

"So?" he said, as little specks of meat flew out onto his chest.

"My God, boy," his mother hissed.

"Don't speak with your mouth *full.*" She leaned across him and patted at his chest with her hankie. "*Disgusting,*" she muttered before turning her attention back to the soap opera.

"How on Earth will you get there, Jonny?" Mr Whitby asked. "It's a two-hour drive from here to the midlands and the navigation system is offline. They're predicting traffic chaos."

"You said I could take the car," Jonny said, jamming the rest of the sausage into his mouth.

Mr Whitby pinched the bridge of his nose. "Yes, I know, Son. I do remember. But there's no navigation system. You'll have to program the directions into the car yourself. Do you know the way from Portsmouth to Wolverhampton?"

Finally, Jonny looked up, and Mr Whitby could see the cogs of his mind clunking into place. The boy hurriedly chewed and swallowed the sausage, keen to avoid another reprimand. "But I have to go, today! I promised to bring Honza with me, *and* it's the last day."

Mrs Whitby rolled her eyes. "Ugh, Honza," she muttered. "He's not coming here, is he? The way he talks with that infernal tool really gets my goat."

"He'll be here any minute, mum. Don't worry, he's not coming in. We were planning on leaving after breakfast."

"Maybe some things were better in the old days then after all, eh?" Mr Whitby said. "I read that people used to have to learn *entire*languages and store them in their *own* memory. Imagine that!"

"Now you sound like your bloody father," Mrs Whitby growled. "That man is a walking anachronism. His obsession with the past is perverse." She got up and stormed to the kitchen, taking the empty breakfast tray with her, muttering her disapproval.

*

Mr Whitby flopped down onto the sofa next to his son. "Don't worry, mate," he said as he wrapped a comforting arm around his shoulder. "You don't have to go and check it out. They'll reserve you a room no matter what."

"You don't understand, Dad," the boy whinged and shrugged his father's arm away.

"They give the best rooms to those who take the time to visit. It's all incredibly old-fashioned, you know. I don't know why we can't just do it online, but they say it shows commitment to the institution or something." He pushed his breakfast away and sank into the sofa. "Now I'm going to get the worst room *ever*."

"We'll think of something," Mr Whitby said, and an idea popped into his mind. "Hang on a minute." He nudged his son in the ribs with a pointy elbow. "Maybe your mother's right about Granddad."

The boy looked almost offended at the name. "Granddad is in a mental hospital, Dad. Or have you forgotten? We used to go there once a year at Christmas, remember? Before Mum forbade it."

"I know, I know, but don't you remember the things he would ramble on about?"

The boy stared at him blank-faced. 'No, no, of course you don't remember, you barely peeled your face from that bloody multitool of yours when we visited."

Jonny made a face. "What's your point, Dad?"

"Before he went into care, your mother

just couldn't stand the fact that he was always trying to give her directions, see? He was convinced that our smart devices weren't infallible and that they might drive her 'off the Eastern Road and into the sea!' Those were his words!" Mr Whitby chuckled to himself at the memory. "Anyway, he used to tell her every time she went to work the correct way to go into the old city of Portsmouth. Your mother used to work there before we got married. It drove her up the wall, it did."

"That why he got sent away?" Jonny asked.

Mr Whitby nodded. "The old coot just never could trust the smart devices we took for granted, even in those days, and he was quite vocal about it. He was an older father, you see? I took his anachronisms as just one of his little quirks, having grown up with them, but your mother saw it differently. When G-Med services got wind of his rantings, they agreed with her wholeheartedly. He's been in that home for twenty-five years. He'll be eighty-five now.' Mr Whitby sighed and slumped into the sofa.

"So, what's your point, Dad?" Jonny said. "Why was Mum right?"

"Well, isn't it obvious?" Mr Whitby said cheerfully. "You can go to the hospital and ask him for directions. He may well know the way to Wolverhampton. When I was a kid, he knew the way everywhere."

Jonny didn't look convinced. "But how could he know? He's just a crazy old man. It's too much information for anyone to remember."

"Don't be so quick to judge, my boy. He didn't care for, or even need, G-Maps like we do. As a younger man, he was the driver for a touring band, pre G-Maps days. He used to drive all over the country. When I was a young boy, I remember he used to brag about it."

"What's to brag about?" the boy said, failing to connect the dots.

"What's to…come on, lad!" Mr Whitby paused a brief moment, hoping in vain his son would fill the silence with the answer. But Jonny just looked at him blankly. "Your Grandfather knew how to drive everywhere!"

The boy perked up in his chair. "Do you really think he could do it?"

"It's been ten years, so I don't know how his mind has held up. He never accepted that the lifetime of knowledge he'd acquired had been rendered useless by technology."

"Maybe not so useless anymore, Dad," Jonny said cheerfully.

Mr Whitby smiled, but the pleasant feeling was quickly drowned by guilt. "I guess he'll be smiling today," he said ruefully.

"But how will I get to the care home, Dad? I still have the same problem. I don't know the way."

"That's easy. It's on the other side of the park, where you used to play football."

'I can walk there in twenty minutes!' Jonny said, standing up.

"Do you want me to come with you?" Mr Whitby asked. "I owe the old man a visit."

Before Jonny could reply, Mrs Whitby's shrill voice pierced their eardrums from the kitchen doorway. "You will not see that crazy old fool, today or ever!" she screeched, emphasizing every word in the sentence. "Sympathising with technology deniers is a very serious crime, and given today's turn of events, do you really want to end up in a care home alongside your father?"

Mr Whitby grimaced. "That's not what I—"

Mrs Whitby held up a hand, cutting him off. "You promised me you'd never see him again."

Mr Whitby sighed. "Yes, dear," he said. He was well aware of the fact his wife was a bitter woman; she wouldn't be the first in the street to have her husband committed. He had to tread carefully. The fact his own father had been committed increased the likelihood of a conviction for himself. "But what about the boy, dear? The old man could help him."

Mrs Whitby's expression softened. "I don't know," she said. "I don't like it, what if he corrupts the—"

She was interrupted by the ringing of her son's multitool.

"It's Honza," Jonny announced desperately. "Please mum, I'll go with him. Dad can stay here with you."

Mr Whitby stared longingly at his wife, who pursed her lips as though she'd just sucked on the world's sourest lemon.

"Let him go," Mr Whitby said. "I'll stay."

Jonny ran to the door and opened it.

"Ahoj Džony," the young Czech said cheerfully. He then peered over Jonny's shoulder into the living room. "A jak se dneska máte paní Chvitbyová?" He held up his multitool, so the speakers faced forward, and a couple of seconds later the translation played out in the same suggestive voice that their fridge had used to speak to Jonny. "*Hi Jonny, and how are you today, Mrs Whitby*?"

"Ugh," she said and waved a hand, ignoring the question completely. "Just go, but don't be long. I don't want you spending any more time than is absolutely necessary with that crazy old man."

"Thanks mum!" Jonny said, but before his father could even ask to send the old man his regards, the boy was out the door.

About the Authors

Syeda Fatima Muhammad

Fatima Taqvi is a writer from Pakistan now living in London. She writes primarily speculative fiction, and her works have appeared in places like Strange Horizons, Flash Fiction Online, and Fusion Fragment magazine. She can be found online on Twitter @FatimaTaqvi, and on her website www.fatimataqvi.com.

Nick Wood

Nick Wood is a disabled South African-British clinical psychologist and Science Fiction (SF) writer, with a collection of short stories (alongside essays and new material) in LEARNING MONKEY AND CROCODILE (Luna Press, 2019). Following AZANIAN BRIDGES (2016), Nick's latest novel is the BSFA shortlisted WATER MUST FALL

(NewCon Press, 2020). Nick can be found at http://nickwood.frogwrite.co.nz/

So Mayer

So Mayer is a writer, bookseller at Burley Fisher Books, and organiser. Their most recent books are the speculative essay A Nazi Word for a Nazi Thing (Peninsula, 2020) and poetry chapbook jacked a kaddish (Litmus, 2018), and their hybrid writing appears in Ghost Calls (DCA, 2021), Magma 79: Dwelling (2021), On Relationships (3ofCups, 2020), At the Pond (Daunt, 2019) and Spells: 21st Century Occult Poetry (Ignota, 2018), and is forthcoming in Extra Teeth 4 and LUMIN. They are currently co-editing an anthology of queer SFFH erotica with Adam Zmith for Cipher Press and Fringe! (Nov 2021).

Jon Bilbao

Jon Bilbao was born in Ribadesella (Asturias, Spain) in 1972 and holds a degree in Mining Engineering and another in English. He is the author of short story collections Como una historia de terror (Salto de Página, 2008), Bajo el influjo del cometa (Salto de Página, 2010), Física familiar (Salto de Página, 2014), Estrómboli (Impedimenta, 2016), and Basilisco (Impedimenta, 2020), and also the novels El hermano de las moscas (Salto de Página, 2008), Padres, hijos y primates (Salto de Página, 2011), Shakespeare y la ballena blanca (Tusquets, 2013), as well as the triptych El silencio y los crujidos (Impedimenta, 2018).

Translator - Mike Lucas

While growing up in Lincoln, England, Mike was surrounded by the favourite books of his older brothers, an extensive collection of writers such as Isaac Asimov, Michael Moorcock and Philip K. Dick, all of whom made a lasting impression.
After studying modern languages at Nottingham University, he moved to Spain, where he trained as a conference interpreter at La Laguna, Tenerife. He combines his

working time between conference interpreting from Spanish, French, Portuguese and Italian into English with translation of all types of texts. He lives in the Penedès wine growing region in Catalonia.

Peter Haynes

Peter Haynes lives and writes in the UK. His debut novel 'The Willow By Your Side' was published by Unsung Stories in 2018, and his short fiction has been published widely online and in print. Find him on Twitter @ManOfZinc.

Michael Crouch

Michael Crouch lives in Norwich where he has worked within the telecommunications business for over 32 years. He has had a number of articles, short stories and comics published in a range of comics and magazines, including the true story of 'Kapitan Fritz's Day Trip to Yarmouth' published in the WW1 anthology, To End All Wars, published by Soaring Penguin Press. In 2019, Michael participated in the University of East Anglia Writing School course, An Introduction to Science Fiction, tutored by the author Ian Nettleton. From work on that course, the kernel of an idea for what became The Trip was born.

Rosie Oliver

Rosie has been in love with science fiction ever since as a teenager she discovered a whole bookcase of yellow-covered Gollancz books in Chesterfield library. It sent her on a world-spinning imaginary journey to having 30 short stories published - one in the Best of British Science Fiction 2020 anthology, being awarded a Silver Honourable Mention and nine Honourable Mentions in the Writers of the Future Contest, and blundering into contributing to a scientific research paper while investigating background stuff for a novel. She is currently concentrating on writing science fiction novels… yes plural, meaning in parallel!

C. John Arthur

C. John Arthur is a British/Swedish citizen, permanently resident in a Stockholm suburb and working by day as a biomedical scientist—chronicled briefly in a past issue of Focus. He's published short fiction in various US-based small press anthologies and is currently doing the final revisions to his first novel, set in a near-future Stockholm. He blogs occasionally on www.blog.cjohnarthur.com.

Gene Rowe

Gene Rowe is an academic and research consultant who has published widely on topics as diverse as forecasting, risk perception, expert knowledge elicitation and public participation in policy making. He also dabbles in sci-fi. His first solo novel - a geopolitical sci-fi thriller entitled 'The Greater Game' - will be published shortly by White Cat Publications (the e-book in September; the paperback in November in the USA, Canada and, of course, via the internet). He is close to completing a second novel - a sci-fi/fantasy hybrid (title still uncertain). Watch this space! 'Here' is his first short story.

Katherine Franklin

Katherine Franklin writes science fiction and fantasy when she isn't writing code and is preparing the first book in her debut space-opera trilogy for publication in early 2022. She spends the rest of her free time on a collection of hobbies, one of which is painting the small mountain of plastic miniatures occupying her cupboards. Only martial arts and her horse-sized dog succeed in dragging her away from her desk. You can find a list of her published work and information about the upcoming trilogy at FranklyWrites.com.

Eugen Bacon & E. Don Harpe

Eugen M. Bacon is African Australian, a computer scientist mentally re-engineered into creative writing. Her work has won, been shortlisted, longlisted or commended in national and international awards, including the Foreword Book of the Year, Bridport Prize, Copyright Agency Prize, Australian Shadows Awards, Ditmar Awards and Nommo Awards for Speculative Fiction by Africans. Her novella Ivory's Story was shortlisted in the BSFA Awards. Upcoming: Danged Black Thing, story collection by Transit Lounge Publishing (2021), Saving Shadows, illustrated microfiction by NewCon Press, and Mage of Fools, an Afrofuturistic dystopian novel by Meerkat Press (2022). Website: eugenbacon.com Twitter: @EugenBacon

E. Don Harpe has had a varied career, from military service in the 1960s to industrial engineering. He is a published Nashville songwriter and a real descendant of the Harpe Brothers, America's first serial killers. Harpe has nearly forty short stories, including two in the Twisted Tales II anthology that won the Eppie Award for best science fiction anthology in 2007. Now retired and living in North Georgia, Harpe devotes his time to

Helen, his wife of more than fifty years, to his children, grandchildren, great-grandchildren, and to his writing.

Elad Haber

Elad Haber is a husband, father to an adorable little girl, and IT guy by day, fiction writer by night. He has 2021 publications from The Daily Drunk, Literally Stories, Sledgehammer Lit, The Night's End Podcast, and in the second print anthology from Brilliant Flash Fiction, Branching Out. You can follow him on twitter @MusicInMyCar or on his website, eladhaber.wordpress.com.

Louis Evans

Louis Evans is the child of lawyers. He hasn't had his phone installed in his skull yet, but it's probably just a matter of time. He wishes everybody a good death.
His work has appeared in Nature: Futures, Interzone, Analog SF&F, and more, and has been longlisted for the BSFA Awards. He is a member of the Clarion West ghost class of the

plague year. He's online at evanslouis.com and tweets @louisevanswrite

Paul Beacon

Paul Beacon is an English teacher and part-time writer from Portsmouth, England.
With fifteen years' experience teaching English as a foreign language behind him, several years ago he decided to put his practical knowledge of grammar and everyday language usage into more creative pursuits.
He began creative writing as a hobby through various online courses and workshops and has been honing his craft ever since. He currently has several pieces of dystopian science-fiction under development, including short stories, novellas, and screenplays.
Paul is currently based in Prague, Czechia and lives with his partner, Daniela and their dog, Poppy.

Printed in Great Britain
by Amazon

79136326R00120